Pressure Play

by Matt Christopher

Illustrated by Karin Lidbeck

Little, Brown and Company

Boston   New York   Toronto   London

To Duane, Karen, and Michelle Elizabeth

Text copyright © 1993 by Matthew F. Christopher
Illustrations copyright © 1993 by Karin Lidbeck

First Paperback Edition

Library of Congress Cataloging-in-Publication Data

Christopher, Matt.
    Pressure play / by Matt Christopher. — 1st ed.
      p.   cm.
    Summary: Travis, less obsessed with baseball than his fellow team members, tries to balance his playing with his hobby of horror videos and starts receiving anonymous threats warning him to spend more time on baseball.
    ISBN 0-316-14098-8 (hc)
    ISBN 0-316-14121-6 (pb)
    [1. Baseball — Fiction.   2. Mystery and detective stories.]
I. Title.
PZ7.C458Pr   1993
[Fic] — dc20   92-37276

10 9 8 7 6 5 4 3 2 1

MV-NY

Published simultaneously in Canada
by Little, Brown & Company (Canada) Limited

Printed in the United States of America

Pressure Play

Team Rosters

Seminoles

1B	Seth Franklin
2B	Howie Lander
3B	Scoot Robertson
SS	Travis Bonelli
RF	Albie Carbone
CF	Chan Lee
LF	Peter Hooper
C	Mert Farish
P	Paul Farley
	Georgie Greene

Pinch hitter

    Jimmy Melville

Swordtails

SS	Stan Weinberg
RF	Zang Blakewell
CF	Andy Reynolds
LF	Karim Kadar
3B	Ron Marino
2B	Terry Wright
1B	Jake Santos
C	Shelly Ross
P	Bobby Meltzer
	Lou Lanahan

Pinch hitter

    Mike Riley

1

Travis Bonelli poured a scoop of soap powder into the dishwasher. He closed the latch and turned the dial.

Kerchug . . . kerchug. The wash cycle began. He looked around the kitchen to make sure it was neat and clean. Then he headed for the back door.

"I'll be out in the garage," he called over his shoulder. "Had your dessert?" his father shouted from the front of the house.

"Yes," Travis replied.

"Done the dishes?"

"Done!" Travis answered brightly.

"What about —"

"Dad, I finished everything," said Travis. He was in a big hurry to leave the house.

Mr. Bonelli walked into the kitchen. A heavyset man, he wore a tight-fitting dark blue T-shirt with *Ken* in yellow threads on the front. In back, it said *Clover Lanes.* That was the name of the bowling

1

alley where he went almost every weekday night.

"Good," he said. "Don't forget to clean the mud out of your cleats. You left them by the back door."

"I scraped them off after I emptied the rubbish," Travis said. "They're up in my closet now. I'm just going over to the garage for a little while, okay?"

"Sure. Wait a minute, are you getting enough rest?" asked Mr. Bonelli. "Got to keep the old body in shape if you want to be a winner."

"I'm doing fine," said Travis. "I had a real good game today. Remember, I told you, we were down —"

"Great," said Mr. Bonelli. "Listen, my bowling team is going to squeeze in a little extra practice tonight, so I have to get going. Matter of fact, I'm already a little late. So make sure the lights are off when you turn in. You should be asleep when I get back. I'll see you in the morning. Oh, if Mom calls, leave me a message about when she's getting back."

Travis's mother was a flight attendant for a big airline. She only worked part of each month, but her job kept her away from home for days at a time. Travis was used to answering calls that came from all over the world.

It was on account of her latest promotion that the Bonellis had moved to Cloverdale, to be near the new international airport. A lot of airline workers lived there.

Mr. Bonelli left before Travis could finish what he had started saying. But that was okay. He'd already told him about the terrific double play he had made that afternoon. It had helped the Cloverdale Seminoles win the first half of the league play-offs.

As he headed toward the garage, Travis smiled. He could still feel the sting of that line drive as it hit the pocket of his glove. With the runner on third base speeding toward home, he had hurled the ball in. It was a perfect throw. The Seminole catcher had nabbed it in plenty of time to make the tag.

That had taken place in the fifth inning. It'd given the Seminoles that little edge they needed to keep them on their toes. The other team got a few hits, but no runs were scored against the Seminoles after that.

Dutch McLane, the Seminoles' coach, had called Travis over after the game. He'd told Travis how pleased he was with his playing. He'd even said that the double play was the turning point in the game.

"Gosh, Coach, thanks," Travis had murmured. But he was really proud of that play.

Some of the guys had razzed him.

"Hall of Fame next, Trav," Paul Farley, the pitcher, had called out.

A bunch of the guys had started a chant: "Tra-vis, Tra-vis." But it soon dissolved in friendly laughter, before his face got bright red.

As soon as he had reached his house, he'd pitched in and helped Mr. Bonelli prepare their dinner.

Ken Bonelli was a great cook. If he hadn't been so successful as a carpenter, he probably could have been a restaurant chef. Travis had no complaints about meals when his mother was out of town.

The only problem was that Mr. Bonelli used a lot of pots and pans. He made a real big mess in the kitchen. And since his father did the cooking, Travis did the cleaning up. Sometimes Mr. Bonelli helped him and they zoomed through the job. But when his father was in a rush to get down to the bowling alley, Travis had to manage on his own.

By the time the kitchen was all spick-and-span, Travis was really wiped out. But he was still charged up by the small package he clutched as he entered the garage.

Travis Bonelli wasn't only a terrific shortstop. He was also a horror movie freak.

He loved all those old gory black-and-white monster films, as well as the latest blood-and-guts thrillers in living color. As soon as he saw the announcement of a new horror movie or a great oldie on television, he couldn't wait to videotape it. Then he could watch it over and over.

But his real hobby was making his own horror videos from his collection of tapes. He carefully picked the best parts and put them together into weird and wacky stories to show all his friends.

That is, he used to show them all the time to his pals — before the Bonellis had moved to Cloverdale. The kids here didn't seem all that interested, except for Peter Hooper, the Seminoles' left fielder. Peter was really more into western movies, but he liked horror, too. He'd howled at the first homemade video Travis had showed him. He'd even said he'd like to see more of them.

But that wasn't the reason Travis was rushing off to the garage that evening. He had something more exciting in mind. The night before, while he'd been watching *Fangs of Frenzy* for the umpteenth time on TV, he'd seen an announcement of a contest for horror movie fans. It was being sponsored by the local video store. All you had to do was send in your best homemade horror video that you'd put together from movie clips. There was a terrific first prize. The winner would get to go to Hollywood to have a small part in a new horror movie. You had ninety days to send in your video.

Travis was really excited about his chances. He had a huge collection of oldies. On each one he had marked the really good scenes. All he had to do was to put together the best.

He thought about telling his folks about the

contest, but he decided it would be more fun to surprise them if he won. As for Peter, well, Travis didn't feel he knew him well enough to get him wound up about a horror video contest.

Besides, there were other things he should be thinking about, like the three-out-of-five championship series that his baseball team would start the very next day. The Swordtails would be a tough team to beat.

His mind wandered back to the game that afternoon. It wasn't only his double play that made him such a valuable player. When he was playing heads-up ball, he seemed to inspire the other guys. The whole team seemed to hit better, to make fewer errors, and to score more runs. There was no question: in his own quiet way, Travis had the makings of a real team leader.

And almost everyone seemed to like him. They were all friendly . . . in a general sort of way. No one became a real pal, except for Peter. It was really different from his old team, where he'd had a lot of close buddies. Maybe after he got to know the new guys better, things would change.

Maybe after he got back from Hollywood!

2

But first he had to get there.

Travis had stopped by the video store on his way home and had picked up a contest entry form. Now, tucked under his arm with the form was a video copy of *The Werewolf's Revenge*. That movie was one of the great horror flicks of all time. It had been shown on TV real late the night before, long after Travis had gone to bed. But he had set the timer on the video recorder and gotten a perfect copy. He could hardly wait to run through it to pick out the best parts.

Travis shut the garage door behind him and headed up the rickety stairs to the unfinished loft. Mr. Bonelli had closed it in with some two-by-fours and plasterboard to form a little workshop for Travis. There was a window for ventilation, and an old raggedy rug in the middle. He'd built a workbench along one wall for Travis's video equipment. Across the room was an old, overstuffed brown leather chair next to a small table that held a remote control switch.

After flicking on the overhead light, Travis went to his workbench. It held his two video monitors, two VCRs, and, between them, his editing controller. The last piece of equipment made it possible to copy individual scenes from a prerecorded videotape onto a blank one.

All this equipment was expensive, but Travis had been able to purchase most of it secondhand. He'd saved the money to pay for it from birthday and Christmas presents. Plus he'd used part of his allowance and the money he got from doing odd jobs. Once his parents had seen how dedicated he was to his hobby, they'd helped pay for the rest. Now he hoarded every penny he could put away to pay for blank tapes.

The contest required a small entry fee, but Travis could come up with that pretty easily. He hadn't bought any new tapes lately, and there was money in his "Horror Fund." He also used that money to see the latest horror movies at the local cinema.

Travis ran his hands lightly over the videotapes

lined up in alphabetical order on the shelf above the equipment. There were no gaps. They were all there.

Then he sat down in the easy chair and looked over the entry form. It said the contest sponsor would send an official application and guidelines after receiving the entry form.

"Name . . . address . . . telephone number . . . age . . ."

With the same felt-tip pen he used to print the labels on his tapes, Travis started to fill in the form in neat block letters.

But he couldn't wait to see *The Werewolf's Revenge*. He slipped it into the playing VCR and turned off the overhead light. Using the remote from the chair, he switched on the tape and adjusted the volume.

"Gargoyle Films proudly presents . . ."

The title came on, followed by a full-screen close-up of the werewolf's face.

Wow, what fangs! Travis shuddered. He snuggled deeper into the chair.

It wasn't long before the action started. A young farmer was attacked by the werewolf and fought back. The way he swung his pitchfork made Travis think of his batting stance. Maybe his legs should be a little farther apart.

The farmer managed to escape the werewolf. He ran to the village church and sounded an alarm by pulling on the church bell.

Brinnnng! Brinnnng!

That wasn't the church bell. It was the telephone!

Travis dashed down the stairs, out of the garage, and into the kitchen. He grabbed the phone on the fifth ring.

"Hello?" he said, puffing a little.

"Travis, is that you?" asked the voice on the other end.

"Peter? Boy, am I ever glad you called. You'll never believe what I'm just starting to watch. Have you ever seen *The Werewolf's Revenge*? I picked up a copy on my way home. And I got an entry form for that contest that —"

"Hold your horses, Travis," Peter Hooper interrupted. "I can't talk about your videos right now. I've got some real exciting news, and I'm calling everyone to tell them about it."

And finally got around to me, Travis thought. I'm the new guy in town, so I'm at the bottom of the list.

"There's a bunch of other guys left after this, so I can't stay on too long," Peter went on. That made Travis feel better.

"What's the big news?" asked Travis.

"Well, you know that new sporting goods store, Hoagy's? Guess what they're going to do?"

"I don't know," said Travis. He wasn't even aware that Hoagy's was a new store in town. It seemed like it had just been there forever when the Bonellis moved to Cloverdale.

"See, they want to drum up business, so they got together with the Parks and Recreation Commission," Peter continued. "They're going to send the team that wins our league championship to the World Series."

"The World Series? The *real* World Series?"

"Right! Wherever it's played," said Peter. "They're going to get us tickets and pay for the whole team to go."

"Wow! How'd you find out?"

"My dad stopped by Hoagy's to pick up his new

bowling ball on his way home and heard about it. It's going to be in the newspaper tomorrow," said Peter. "So I figured I ought to tell the guys tonight so we can get ready. We have to play heads-up ball tomorrow."

"Sure we do," said Travis.

"And everyone will be counting on our ace shortstop, Travis Bonelli, to do his stuff," said Peter. "Like that terrific double play in the fifth today. That was really something. A few like that tomorrow and we'll be golden."

"Sure thing," said Travis. "I'm just going to finish watching this video. And then maybe run it through to mark the parts I want to use —"

He was all set to let Peter in on the contest. But he was interrupted again by the voice on the other end of the phone. "Maybe you ought to knock off the video stuff tonight and get some rest. You're going to need it tomorrow."

Why is everyone bugging me about rest all of a sudden? Travis thought. "I will, I will, Peter. Don't worry about me."

"Great, Travis. See you tomorrow," said Peter.

Travis hung up the phone and went back to the

garage. Maybe I ought to skip the werewolf movie, he thought. Probably wouldn't be such a bad idea to get some rest. After all, I really don't want to disappoint the team.

Travis took the video out of its slot and placed it at the end of the shelf. He shut off all the equipment, switched off the light, and left the workshop.

On his way to his bedroom, he glanced at the TV in the living room.

Gee, is there anything on the Monster Movie Channel tonight? he wondered.

He flicked on the TV and found the channel. It was an oldie he'd seen a zillion times. But there was a good part coming up.

Travis settled down on the living room couch, his eyes glued to the TV set. I have this on tape already, he thought, but maybe I'll see something I can use for the contest.

The exciting part came and went. The clock on the mantel ticked away the minutes. Travis's eyelids drooped, then finally closed.

3

There was a lady on the telephone. She was shouting at a werewolf who hovered over her. Why didn't she just put down the phone and talk to him? And why was she calling the werewolf Travis?

"Travis! Travis, I can't believe you're still up. You're going to be a wreck tomorrow if you don't get some sleep!"

It wasn't the lady or the werewolf calling his name — it was his father.

Travis leaped up from the couch and stretched. Then he hurried over to the TV and shut it off.

"We took the TV out of your bedroom," said Mr. Bonelli, "but it looks like you just changed the place you fall asleep. Maybe we should move your bed down here."

Travis laughed. "Sort of like the old treehouse I used to have back home," he said.

"Yeah, well, this is our home now," said Mr.

15

Bonelli. He fluffed up the sofa cushions. "I'm really starting to get used to it, aren't you?"

Without waiting for an answer, he went on: "I'm sure glad you suggested I join that bowling league. I've met a lot of nice guys, including Bernie Hooper. I guess his son, Peter, plays for the same team you do."

"Uh-huh, Peter plays left field," said Travis. "He just called a little while ago. Say, did Mr. Hooper tell you about Hoagy's Sports Shop?"

"I know he got a new bowling ball there today," said Mr. Bonelli. "I'm glad mine is in good shape. Really important to have the right equipment. And to take care of it. Did you put your cleats away, Travis?"

"I told you I did, Dad," said Travis. "But there's something I just found out. I thought Mr. Hooper might have said something to you about it. About the offer Hoagy's made."

"No, we didn't really get a chance to talk," said Mr. Bonelli. "The team before us finished early, so we got right down to practice. What's going on?"

16

Travis told him about the announcement that was going to be in the papers the next day.

"The World Series? That's wonderful, Travis," said Mr. Bonelli. "Of course, you have to win your own championship series first. When is the first game?"

"Tomorrow," Travis replied.

"Tomorrow? And you're still up? How do you expect to be in top shape if you stay up till all hours? Don't you want to go to the World Series?"

"Sure," said Travis. "I take care of myself. Don't I eat right?"

"It takes more than just eating right," said Mr. Bonelli. "You have to maintain a balance in your life. You need exercise, a proper diet, and rest, too."

"Right," said Travis.

"So I suggest you head upstairs right now and get some shut-eye," said his father. "I'll be up myself in a few minutes."

For the first time, Travis noticed that his father had put down a videotape next to the TV.

"Are you going to watch a video now?" Travis asked. "What about your rest?"

"As a matter of fact, this is a tape one of the guys on the bowling team shot at practice tonight. I'm just going to take a look at my run-up to make sure I have it right. I felt a little off stride," said Mr. Bonelli.

"Just make sure you don't stay up too late," said Travis, with a sly grin.

He dashed up the stairs, just in time to dodge the small pillow his father threw at him.

4

The ball touched down on the green grass about a foot in front of him. Travis bent over, scooped it up, and threw it to Howie Lander at second base. Howie tagged the runner out and pegged the ball home. Mert Farish, the Seminoles' catcher, pulled it in, but the run had already scored.

As the Swordtails' fans cheered, third baseman Scoot Robertson trotted over to Travis.

"What's the matter with you, Travis? The play was at home!" he said angrily. "There was plenty of time. Now look at the score!"

The scoreboard read 3–1.

It was only the bottom of the third inning, but the Seminoles had enjoyed a healthy 3–0 lead until then. Now, with one run in and men on first and third, their comfortable lead was threatened.

Travis didn't say anything. He just scuffed the ground with his right foot and slammed his fist into his glove. Up until that play, he'd really helped the Seminoles a lot. He had belted out a double that had brought one base runner home, plus he'd knocked in a single that had ended up going the distance on a Swordtail error.

But on the field, his mind had wandered. When the last ball came his way, he'd been thinking about the contest entry form he had popped into the mailbox that morning.

Paul Farley, on the mound for the Seminoles, called over to them, "C'mon you guys. Let's play some ball!"

Scoot went back to his position as play resumed.

The next Swordtail batter was their best hitter, left fielder Karim Kadar. Coach Dutch McLane signaled his Seminole outfield to play him deep. Travis and Howie skipped back a few steps, too. So far Kadar had struck out once and then slugged a long, deep hit into the Seminole outfield. But Peter Hooper had made a terrific save at the back wall for the out.

The Seminole pitcher nodded, wound up, and sped the ball toward the plate.

Kadar's bat connected for a line drive between second and short. Travis raced for the ball, but there was no way he could snag it in the air. By going deep for it, he managed to hold the hit to a single. The runner on first advanced to second base. But the third base occupant decided that the distance to the plate was too far and stayed put.

Bases loaded and only one out, thought Travis. Oh, brother, what a mess. He blinked his eyes a couple of times to clear his brain and looked over at the plate.

Swordtail third baseman Ron Marino had walked his first time at bat. He'd struck out on his second attempt. But he was a top performer during the regular season. He couldn't be taken for granted.

Travis could see Paul Farley sweating. His white uniform with skinny blue stripes and a big blue number on the back was soaked.

Concentrate, thought Travis. Paul has to concentrate. So do I, for that matter.

His thoughts were interrupted by a shout from third baseman Scoot Robertson: "Let's go, Paulie-boy!"

The Seminole infield chimed in after him.

"Easy out!"

"Put 'im away, Farley!"

"Show him some steam!"

Farley's first pitch was a fastball, right down the middle.

Marino swung — and missed it.

"Strike one!" called the umpire.

The next pitch just managed to catch the outside corner for a called strike.

Paul threw a couple of high and outside pitches to make the count 2 and 2.

Travis had to keep blinking and skipping around in place to keep his mind alert. He felt sluggish, and his eyelids wanted to droop.

Crack!

Farley's pitch had been a little high, but Marino had gone for it. The ball connected with the topside of the bat, popping off a skyscraper. It looked like it would land halfway between the pitcher's mound and the shortstop position.

"It's all yours, Travis!" called Scoot from third.

Travis captured the ball and pegged it home so fast that it stung Mert's hand. But the Seminole catcher was on his toes and managed to hurl the ball down to Scoot, who tagged the runner before he could get back to the base. It was the final out.

"Nice going, Travis," said Scoot as the team came off the field. "Another double play just when we really needed it."

Travis just nodded and adjusted his cap. But Mert Farish sneered loudly, "Yeah, but whose fault was it that we had the bases loaded, anyhow?"

"Knock it off, you guys," said Coach McLane. "Who's up first?" he asked.

"It's the top of the order," answered a blond girl chewing gum at the far end of the bench. "Seth leads off. Howie, you're on deck."

The gum-chewing girl was Steffi McGory, a real baseball nut. She played first base for the Rockettes in the Cloverdale Girls' Baseball League. Even though her team had finished their season with a winning record, they'd only come in fourth place. She was such a regular fan at Seminole games, Coach McLane had made her the official scorekeeper for the play-offs. He knew he could count on her. Steffi never made a mistake. Her scorecard at the end of the game was as clean as a whistle.

As first baseman Seth Franklin took a few practice swings, Travis nudged Peter, who was sitting next to him.

"Guess I'm a little tired," he admitted. "I probably should have gone to bed earlier. But I had to go through this werewolf tape 'cause —"

"Wait a sec, Trav," said Peter. "I want to see how Seth does."

The tall, red-headed Franklin wasn't doing too well. The count was 0 and 2.

Even though the next pitch was outside, Seth stepped into it. He would have connected if his swing wasn't high. He woofed it for the out.

As he passed Seth on his way to the on-deck circle, Scoot Robertson called over, "No sweat, buddy. You'll get 'im next time."

Nobody says that to me, thought Travis. Whenever I do something wrong, I hear about it. Especially from Mert. What's his beef, anyhow?

As Travis sat there thinking about Mert, he hardly noticed Howie Lander take first base on a walk.

24

"You're on deck, Travis," said Steffi, snapping her gum. "Heads up."

On the second pitch to him, Scoot Robertson hit a line drive to the second baseman, who put it away for the second out. Lander held at first.

Travis stepped up to the plate and looked out at the field. He counted off each Swordtail player in their gray uniforms with their red trim. The dirt tracks to the bases and the broad field of gleaming green grass stared back at him.

He loved this moment every time he came up to bat. It was him and his bat against the ball, the pitcher, and the whole opposing team.

Whoosh!

The first pitch was way inside. Travis bowed back from it and glared at the pitcher.

The next two pitches were balls, too.

"He's afraid of you, Travis!" called a voice from the dugout. Was one of the guys cheering him on? He glanced over and saw Peter give him the high-sign.

The next pitch came sizzling down the middle. Travis swung.

Kerrrrack!

The ball rose high into the sky over center field, deeper and deeper and deeper — and over the fence. Home run!

Howie sped around the bases. Travis followed him at a slower pace.

At home plate, the whole team greeted the runners. Several players even gave Travis high fives. But some of them held off.

Coach McLane gave him a pat on the back.

"Nice work," said the coach. "Okay, you guys, let's keep it going."

But Bobby Meltzer, the Swordtails' pitcher, kept his cool. After two strike calls, Seminole right fielder Albie Carbone grounded out to first base.

As his team ran out to the field, Travis felt a little better than when he had come in to the dugout. Hitting that home run might make the guys forget his fielding mistake. Besides, maybe it wasn't a mistake. Maybe it was — what did the TV sportscasters call it? — a judgment call. Yeah, that was it.

He yawned.

Farley was revved up by the Seminoles' lead.

He struck out the first two Swordtails with six straight pitches. The third out came on a high fly ball that landed smack in the middle of Peter Hooper's glove.

"You're up, Chan," called Steffi as the Seminoles scrambled into the dugout. "No rest for you, Pete," she added. "You're on deck."

The Seminole center fielder, Chan Lee, strode out to the plate. Thin and wiry, he wasn't a power hitter. He was, however, the fastest runner on the team. He could be counted on for extra bases if he got a hit.

Chan belted out an easy single on a line drive down the third base line. He couldn't quite stretch it to second base.

"Come on, Peter, send him home," called Steffi, looking up from her scorecard.

But Peter went down on a called strike after popping up five consecutive foul balls toward first base.

As the Seminole left fielder walked back to his spot on the bench, Coach McLane said to him, "Relax a little, Peter. You're so tight, you're pulling in. That's why you're hitting so many foul balls."

"Thanks, Coach," Peter murmured. He slumped down on the bench.

Mert Farish followed him at the plate. The Swordtail pitcher walked Mert. That put a second man on base. But Paul Farley, the next batter, was an easy out.

Then the top of the Seminole batting order, Seth Franklin, came up.

Meanwhile, Travis tried to help his pal Peter lighten up. He started to talk about the old movie he'd seen the night before on TV.

"It was called *Sorry, Wrong Number,* and it was all about this lady who really needed help. Only she couldn't get through on the phone. She kept hearing these strange conversations between people she didn't know. Or she thought she didn't know them. And it got scarier and scarier — "

"Take a break, Travis," Peter snapped. "We're here to play a ball game. Remember what's at stake."

Travis felt like he'd been hit by a wet towel.

Mert Farish had been listening to them and added his two cents' worth. "Yeah, Bonelli," he chimed in, "maybe you ought to keep your mind on the game instead of those dumb TV movies of yours. I could've nailed that guy in the third if you'd've made the play at home like you should've."

Travis turned bright red.

But Peter sprang to his defense. "I don't see any error on the scoreboard," he snapped back at Mert.

"Are you guys here to play ball or what?" asked Steffi. "What's all this gab about movies and past history? Look at what's going on now. There's a full count on Seth." She snapped her gum and turned toward the plate.

Everyone was used to Steffi mouthing off, but this time she'd gotten their attention. They leapt to their feet and shouted out to the batter.

"Sock it to 'im!"

"Over the fence! All the way!"

"Come on, Seth! Show 'em what you've got!"

With the whole team rooting for him, Seth wobbled a little grounder to the mound that made for an easy out at first.

The score remained 5–1.

It didn't stay that way for long. With his team

up by four runs, Paul Farley seemed to have lost his best stuff. He walked the first two batters at the start of the bottom of the fifth. That wouldn't have been so bad, but the Swordtail batters were starting to show their strength. After a pop-up for the first out, a hot grounder through the hole between first and second loaded the bases.

Karim Kader, the Swordtails' strongest hitter, strode to the plate. Paul threw two balls, then a sizzling fastball to put the count at 2 and 1. Paul's next pitch was right down the middle, and Karim swung hard.

Crack!

Travis's heart sank as he watched the ball soar into the sky and then over the fence. A grand slam homer! The Swordtail fans went wild as Karim followed his teammates around the bases.

The score was now tied at 5–5.

Fortunately for the Seminoles, the next two Swordtail batters didn't follow Karim's lead. Ron Marino grounded out, and Terry Wright went down swinging.

At the top of the sixth and final inning, the score remained Seminoles 5, Swordtails 5.

5

Travis felt as though he had been playing a doubleheader. There was no question that his lack of rest had affected his playing. Luckily, he hadn't been called on to do much fielding. The Seminoles had confined their hitting to the first-base and right-field side of the ballpark. The few plays that had come his way had been easy outs.

But now every move counted. He had to play razor-sharp ball. Peter was right: there was no time to think of the horror video contest, or werewolves, or frightening phone calls on a TV movie. The action was live and right in front of him.

Paul Farley led off. He had gone 0 for 2, and the Swordtails probably had him figured for an easy out. Meltzer threw a fastball down the middle for a called strike. Then he eased off a little. His next pitch was a real meatball, and Farley ate it up. He took a powerful swing and connected for a clean hit that flew out to deep center field.

31

By the time Andy Reynolds, the Swordtail out-
fielder in the middle, caught up with it, Paul was
safe and sound on second base.

That brought up Seth, who was still looking to
make his mark.

"You can do it, Seth!" shouted Peter. He'd kept
his seat next to Travis, but he hadn't talked much
since he'd struck out in the fourth.

Come on, Franklin! Travis added silently.

The rest of the team chimed in with Peter.

The cheering must have gotten to Seth. It
helped pull him out of his slump. He slammed a
line drive between second and short that got him
to first safe and moved Paul to third.

With two runners on base, Howie Lander came
up to bat. He'd had a pretty mixed time of it at
the plate, but he was always a threat. The Swordtail outfield played him deep.

Meltzer took his time reading his catcher's sig-
nals. He picked the third offering.

Meltzer wound up and hurled a curve that
broke just inside at the last second. It was a pitch
Howie liked. He swung at it and popped it high

toward the third base line — on the wrong side. A foul. Strike one.

That was followed by a swing and a miss for strike two. And finally, a called strike for the first Seminole out of the inning.

Scoot Robertson was up next.

Steffi drummed her pencil on the scorecard as the tension rose.

Travis moved to the on-deck circle.

As he took a few practice swings, he started thinking about the scene from *The Werewolf's Revenge* when the farmer had swung the pitchfork like a baseball bat. He was so caught up in his thoughts, he didn't realize Scoot Robertson had flied out. Then he heard Steffi call to him. She pointed at home plate and scowled.

Travis took a couple more practice swings, tugged at the brim of his batting helmet, and stepped to the plate.

Bobby Meltzer scowled as his catcher, Shelly Ross, offered him a choice of pitches.

He led off with a fastball, down the middle.

Luckily, Travis was ready for it. He hit the ball

just deep enough into the outfield to drive Paul home. The scoreboard now read 6–5.

Travis was safe on first, and Seth had moved up to second base. But they never got any farther. Albie Carbone popped out to the third baseman to retire the Seminoles for the inning.

"Thanks for the ride home, Travis," said Paul as the team moved onto the field. "I usually don't see the plate from that angle."

Travis smiled, but he wasn't all that cheerful. Peter was the only one on the team to congratulate him openly on his hit. The rest of the guys had cheered loudly, but no one said a word to him.

Maybe they think I can do that every time, like some kind of baseball machine! he thought.

It looked as though Paul's run home had worn him out a little. He walked the first batter.

"Settle down, Paulie," called Howie from second base.

"Easy does it," shouted Seth at first.

Travis just nodded and scuffled around halfway between second and third.

The next two Swordtail batters were so hungry

for a hit, they swung at anything Paul threw. Both struck out in quick succession.

With a man on first and two away, Stan Weinberg, the Swordtail shortstop, came up to hit. He had walked his last time at bat. However, Coach McLane had advised the team to play deep when Stan was at bat because he had belted a long ball to center field in the first inning. Chan Lee had just managed to grab it before it hit the fence.

Travis watched Stan pop off a couple of foul balls, but then his mind wandered again from the game to the horror video contest. Suddenly he realized that his teammates were yelling at him. He looked up just in time to see Stan connect with the ball. Too late, Coach McLane's advice flashed through his brain.

The ball landed about ten feet behind Travis.

He scrambled back for the ball as the runner on first came speeding by second on his way to third base. Stan was hot on his heels.

Travis tried to make the play at third, but his throw was wild. There was no way Scoot could catch that ball. He leaped at it, but it bounced off

the tip of his glove. By the time he got a hold of the ball, Stan was on his way toward home plate. Scoot made a valiant try, but his throw was too late.

Both runners had scored, giving the game to the Swordtails. Final score: Swordtails 7, Seminoles 6.

"An infield home run! Rats!" snarled Mert Farish. "I can't believe it!"

No one felt worse than Travis.

"It's all my fault," he said to Coach McLane when he came off the field. "I should have played him deep."

"Didn't you remember my warning?" the coach asked.

"I guess I forgot it," Travis said. "I should have known enough, anyhow."

"Well, you had a great game at bat, Travis," said Coach McLane. "Couldn't ask for much more there. But you have to keep your wits about you out on the field, too."

Travis just sighed and headed for the dugout to pick up his stuff. Nobody said much to him as he picked up his bat and bundled up his jacket.

The guys paired off in twos and threes as they walked off the field. One of the last to go was Peter. He had started to leave with Seth but turned for a minute and said to Travis, "Hey, it's only the first game. We can still win the series. Just have to dig in, I guess."

"I feel rotten about that last hit," Travis admitted quietly. "I don't know why I didn't play him deeper."

"Look, it happens," said Peter. "Go on, Seth," he called out. "I'll catch up in a minute. Trav, you just have to concentrate more next time. Don't get so uptight."

"You're right," Travis said. "I'm going to put away my glove when I get home and just relax. Maybe I'll do some work on my special new video."

"The one with the werewolf?" Peter asked.

"That's just part of it," said Travis. "I have this terrific oldie about Blackbeard the Pirate I'm going to put in. He makes his victims salute the pirate flag before they walk the plank."

"Sounds pretty good," said Peter. "When do I get to see it?"

"You really want to?" said Travis. "It's kind of rough right now. I have a lot of work to do on it, but, uh, I could show you most of it tomorrow."

"Sounds good to me," said Peter. "I'll be around my house tomorrow."

"Great," said Travis. "I'll bring it over."

"Seth's waiting, so I'd better get a move on," said Peter. "Don't forget, Trav, take it easy. We want our star hitter ready for the next game."

Travis noticed that Peter hadn't called him "star shortstop," the way he usually did.

As the last Seminole disappeared down the road, Travis started for home.

He was really miserable now. Even though the other guys hadn't said anything, he knew how they felt. He had let them down. But what did they want from him, anyhow? He had given it his best shot. All they seemed to care about was that he make every play that came his way and then go in and get one hit after another. And when the game was over? Huh, they could care less about him!

"Tag! You're it now," said a voice from behind.

He looked over his shoulder and saw Steffi. He

had been so lost in his thoughts, he hadn't heard her footsteps behind him.

"I'm not in the mood for games," he said.

"I know — I saw the last one you played," she said sarcastically. But before he could reply, she quickly added, "Just kidding. Don't look so gloomy, Travis. It could have been a lot worse if the Seminoles didn't have your hitting. Now, this is what I think —"

"Whoa! Stop!" he protested. "Give it a break for a minute. Don't you ever think about anything besides baseball?"

"What else is there?" she answered, laughing at him.

Should I tell her about the contest? he wondered. He decided to test the water.

"Well, for one thing, there's movies," he said. "And videos."

"Videos! Travis, you've got to lay off that stuff. I heard you talking to Peter, and really! Just concentrate on your fielding more. Now, in the fourth inning . . ."

He shook his head. There was no way he was going to change Steffi. It was baseball or nothing.

6

The next day, when Mrs. Bonelli called, Travis was feeling a lot better. He'd gotten a good night's sleep, and he'd put the disappointing first game of the series behind him.

"Wait until you hear this, Mom," he started to say as soon as he heard her voice. "You know that new sports shop, Hoagy's?"

"Travis, please, I haven't even heard how you and your father are," she said over the phone. "Are you both all right?"

"Of course, we're just hunky-dory," he said. "Why shouldn't we be?"

"Well, your father is so wrapped up with his bowling league," she said. "I sometimes wonder if it was such a great idea for him to rush into that so soon after we moved."

"Oh, Mom, he loves bowling, and he's met some great guys," said Travis. I wish I could say the same, he thought. "But I have two big things to tell you. One's this contest, see, and the other's about the World Series."

"The World Series? That's not till the fall, Travis," said Mrs. Bonelli. "Oh, there's the call for my flight. I'd better hurry. I'll call you from my next stop. I love you."

Click.

I love you, too, Mom, he thought. I just wish you weren't always in such a hurry. Oh, well, I might as well go work on my contest video. I won't tell Peter about the contest until after he sees it. Then, I'll get a —

Brinnng! Brinnng!

Gee, maybe that's Mom calling back, he guessed. Maybe her flight got cancelled and she wants to hear about the two things I started to tell her about.

He picked up the receiver and answered cheerfully, "Bonelli residence. Travis Bonelli at your service!"

"*Mahhmmmuhnub!*" said the voice at the other end of the line. Travis couldn't make out the actual words, but he knew it wasn't his mother talking.

"Sorry, I didn't get that," he said. "Would you mind repeating what you said?"

This time the voice was a little clearer. It sounded as though it said, "Smarten up! Square away your fielding . . . or else!" And then the line went dead.

Who the heck could that have been? Travis thought. One of the guys playing a joke? Nah, he decided. Probably just a wrong number.

Besides, even if it wasn't a wrong number, there was no sense taking something dumb like that seriously. Especially when he had something important to do, like working on that contest video.

As he headed for the garage, he noticed yesterday's newspaper on the kitchen table.

Might as well dump that on the recycling pile, he figured, picking it up.

His eye caught an ad on the movie page.

"Wow!" he exclaimed out loud. *The Return of the Scum Creature, Part II!* I didn't know that was playing!"

Brinnng! Brinnnng!

Maybe this time it's Mom again. Or the wise guy.

"Hello? Oh, hi, Steff, I thought you were . . . never mind. What's up?"

"Travis, are you okay? You sound kind of weird," Steffi asked over the phone. "Are you still out of it from yesterday?"

"Steffi, please, give me a break, huh?" he pleaded. "What's really on your mind?"

"I just wanted to know if you felt like throwing the old ball around. You know, keep in shape," she said. "I mean, I was just in the neighborhood, you know, and since the light in your workshop wasn't on, I figured you weren't doing anything special. Am I right?"

"You're right, Steffi," he said, smiling. "And you're *always* in the neighborhood. You live just around the corner."

"Right, so I could be over in a minute," she said.

"Well, there's this movie I'd really like to see, and it's playing down at the mall," he said. "Tell you what, Steff, it's about time you took a movie break. I'll make a deal. You can loosen up your arm by throwing some high fly balls for me to catch — and then we'll go to the movies. What do you say?"

"You've got yourself a deal, Travis!"

A few minutes later, Travis was craning his neck. He stared into the sky to pick out Steffi's toss.

She kept up a running play-by-play, just like an announcer on television.

"It's a long, high, deep, long —"

"You said 'long' already," he shouted back as the ball dropped into his glove.

"Well, it was *very* long," she called out to him.

"One more and that's it," he answered back. "We don't want to be late for the movie."

"What are we going to see, anyhow?" she asked.

"You'll find out," he said.

She hurled the ball high into the air. "Okay, this time it's an easy pop-up down the third base line, and Travis Bonelli, Old Mr. Reliable, is going, going . . . and he has it for the out."

Travis tossed his glove and ball into the garage, and they headed off to the mall.

The Cloverdale Multiplex offered a choice of six different first-run feature films. Travis wasn't interested in the others, but Steffi surprised him. She knew a lot about the movies after all.

"That one's a mushy love story. Yuck!" she said. "And that one's a pirate movie. Oh, there's one in French with the words on the bottom. I hate those. Oh, and there's one about that cute puppy that moves into the barn with the baby lambs."

"Talk about 'yuck'!" Travis said. "Let's get into line so we can get good seats for *Scum Creature*."

Two hours later, they staggered out of the movie theater.

"Wow, that was really scary!" said Steffi.

"Yeah, it was almost as good as the first *Scum Creature*," said Travis.

He wondered if he would ever be able to make a movie as good as that. When you came right down to it, his own videos were pretty amateur-ish. Where did he get off entering one in a contest? The judges will probably laugh at it.

"I'm not going to offer you a penny for your thoughts, Travis," said Steffi. "'Cause you look the same as you did in the last inning yesterday — you know, kind of lost in space."

"I've got a lot on my mind," he admitted. "Not just the play-offs. You see, I'm entering one of my videos in this horror movie contest. At least, I think I'm going to, if I can fix it up so that it's better than it is right now. And I'm trying to keep in shape so I can play my best game and so we can win the play-offs and go to the World Series — even if I don't end up going after all."

"What do you mean, you won't go? Why not?"

"'Cause I probably wouldn't have that good a time," he said quietly. "After all, who am I going to hang around with? Peter will probably spend all his time with Seth or someone. There's no one else who has any time for me."

"So what am I, chopped liver?" Steffi said, sharply. "Look, Travis, in case you haven't noticed, I'm as good a pal as there is. And I don't like being taken for granted."

"I'm sorry, Steff," he admitted. "I really didn't mean it that way."

"*I* know you didn't, Travis, but someone else might not," she said seriously. "When's this con-

47

test, anyway? Do you have to send something in?"

"Not for another eighty-eight days," he said. "I'm still waiting to get the official application and guidelines."

Steffi groaned. "You have plenty of time to work on your videos — after the play-offs! Get your priorities straightened out, okay? Just wise up!"

Wise up! Just like that joker on the phone said. Steffi would get a laugh out of hearing about that.

But just then Steffi spotted someone in the crowd. "Hey, look who's coming out of the puppy movie. It's Mert Farish. Hey, Mert!" she shouted.

The Seminole catcher was surprised to hear his name called. But he recognized Steffi's voice — probably from all the yelling she did at the ballpark.

He started to walk toward her. When he saw Travis, he almost changed his direction.

"Hey, Mert, how'd you like that puppy movie?" she asked.

Mert turned slightly red. He seemed embar-

rassed that he was caught coming from a kids'
movie.

"Ah, it was okay," he mumbled.

"We didn't see that one. We went to *Scum
Creature, Part II*," said Travis.

"Well, goody for you," scoffed Mert. "Two little
palsy-walsies going to the movies together. A real
dynamic duo, you two!"

Steffi laughed. "Yeah, Travis just swept me off
my feet. Who could resist an offer to sit through
Scum Creature, Part II?"

"Yeah, well, when you start out with one weird
creature, what's the big deal going to see another?" said Mert.

"What's that supposed to mean?" asked Travis.

"Don't go getting hot under the collar," Steffi
scolded. "We're just talking about movies here,
guys. So tell me about the puppy, Mert, was he
really cute?"

Just movies, thought Travis. All she usually
talks about is baseball. But she's blabbing away
with him about some silly puppy movie. Look at
the two of them. Instant pals. I could hit three
grand slams in a row, and I still wouldn't make

49

any new friends, but all she has to do is talk about a dog! And with someone who's always on my case.

As Steffi and Mert rattled on, Travis wandered away from the movie theater and the mall.

The heck with them. The heck with everyone, he decided. I'll just go my way — make my video and enter the contest. And I'll keep on playing just like a regular baseball machine. After all, isn't that what everyone wants me to do?

7

When Travis returned home, he checked the house before going up to his workshop. There was a note on the kitchen table.

"Gone bowling. There's a casserole and some salad in the fridge. Nuke the casserole, and have some fruit for dessert. I'll probably see you later. And don't spend all day and all night in your workshop. Love, Dad."

Travis decided he'd eat after he got back from Peter's house. He couldn't wait to get a reaction to his contest video, or as far as he'd gotten with it. He decided to take a few others with him. Peter had never seen some of his earliest efforts.

On his way out, Travis stuck a ripe banana in his back pocket. Just in case I get hungry before I attack the casserole, he thought.

Brinnnng! Brrinngggg!

The phone, just as he was on his way.

"Okay, okay, I'm coming," he said as he put down the tapes. "Hello?"

The voice was muffled, but he could make out the words right off: "Don't waste your time. Concentrate on your game. Or else!"

"Say, who is this? What's the —"

Click.

The phone went dead.

It has to be some kind of nut, he thought. Who would want to pester me like that? Who cares that much about what I do, anyhow?

Peter lived just a short distance from the Bonelli house. Travis grabbed his videos and was at the corner of his street in less than ten minutes. He could see the Hoopers' white-frame house with the big maple tree and the tall green hedges in front. It looked pretty quiet.

Travis walked down the driveway to the back door, the one he always used when he visited Peter. He rang the bell. There was no answer. He waited a few minutes and then rang again. Still no answer.

The side door to the garage had four little windows. Travis could see that the garage was empty.

Rats! he thought, starting down the driveway. I should have called first. But Peter said he'd be home all day, didn't he? So why isn't he there now? Just my luck.

Lost in his thoughts, Travis didn't see the bicycle coming down the street until it was almost upon him.

"Watch out!" shouted a voice.

Travis leaped over to one side and fell into the hedges. His stack of videotapes went flying. They landed all over the sidewalk.

"Why don't you watch where you're going?" called Mert Farish from the bicycle.

"Why don't you!" Travis shouted angrily. "You could've killed someone. They ought to lock you up!"

He got up and rubbed his backside. The banana was crushed flat in his back pocket. It oozed out the top.

"Well, you're just lucky I didn't run right into you," said Mert. Then a look of genuine concern crossed his face. "You're not hurt, are you?" he asked.

"I'm just fine," Travis sputtered. "No thanks to you!"

"Ah, go jump in the lake!" snarled Mert. He turned to pedal away, but then his eyes fell on the crushed banana. "What's that you got in your back pocket, Bonelli? A banana split? Ha, ha!" And off he went.

Travis tried to clean up his pants with his handkerchief. Then he turned his attention to the scattered videotapes, when he heard someone call from the other direction.

"Travis! What's going on?" shouted Peter. "I was just going to call you. Why are all these tapes all over the ground?" He bent over to help Travis pick them up.

Grumbling as he whisked away some dirt from the tapes, Travis told Peter his version of what had happened.

"I'm sure Mert followed me here and then tried to run me down," he said.

Peter shook his head. "I doubt that," he said.

"Oh, yeah? He's always taking cheap shots at me," said Travis. "I bet he's even been making these dumb phone calls I've been getting." Travis told Peter what the muffled voice had said.

"Travis, are you getting one of your horror movies mixed up with real life?" asked Peter with a smile on his face. "I think you're making a big deal out of nothing. I'm telling you, it was probably just a coincidence that Mert was here. He lives nearby, and he rides his bike around here all the time."

"Hah!"

"Look, no one got hurt," said Peter. "And here are the tapes. We've got *Travis's Tales of Terror, Part One, Part Two,* and *Part Three.* And, let's see, there's *Crypt Creatures, Monsters of the Marsh,* and, what's this, *W.I.P.?* Shouldn't it be *R.I.P.?*"

"No, it's right," said Travis. "It stands for *Work in Progress.* It's the one I'm putting together from all the others — plus a few more, like the werewolf movie."

"Great!" said Peter. "We can really get into the horror scene with this batch. Let's go settle down and watch a few. Maybe it will help you relax so you can concentrate on the game."

"The game?"

"Yeah, you know, the second game in the series

with the Swordtails? Gosh, don't tell me you forgot?"

"No, I was just kidding," said Travis hastily.

"Whew! That's a good thing," said Peter. "Remember, the team's counting on you."

Sure they are, thought Travis. They want the machine to run smoothly. But he didn't tell Peter that. Instead, he asked, "By the way, where were you just now? I thought you were going to be around all day."

"I went out to get some microwave popcorn. Can't watch a movie without popcorn, can you?" Peter suddenly stopped and sniffed. He wrinkled his nose. "Say, Trav, is it my imagination, or do you smell like a ripe banana?"

At the start of the next game, Travis could feel the tension in the air. During the warm-up, there were wild throws and a lot of fumbling around. The team was really wound up. Just before the game started, Coach McLane called everybody together.

"You guys have all the stuff you need to win this

game," he told them. "Forget about the World Series. Forget about the rest of our series. Just think about this game, today. The rest will take care of itself."

"Sounds pretty good to me," said Howie. He was sitting next to Travis on the bench, tightening his laces. "You all set to play ball, Trav?"

Travis nodded.

"Good, just make sure you don't 'go ape' out there," said Howie. He doubled over laughing. Travis saw Mert was grinning, too.

Mert must have said something about the banana! It couldn't have been Peter. But Howie had said, "Make sure you don't . . ." That sounded like a threat. Could Howie be the mystery caller?

Travis was determined not to let anything get to him. He was going to play just like a machine, that's all.

The whistle blew, and the Seminoles took to the field. Georgie Greene tossed the ball to Travis, who automatically pegged down the line to Seth at first base. The ball circulated a few more times and ended up with Travis. The Seminole shortstop thought about throwing a sizzler to Mert, who didn't look as though he were expecting it. But he cooled off and flipped the ball to Georgie on the mound.

Stan Weinberg, the Swordtails' shortstop, led off with a pop fly right to Seth, who packed it away for the out.

Georgie held his own against the next two batters. He retired them with easy strikeouts.

Steffi called over to Travis when he came into the dugout. "Nice and easy, huh? Went like clockwork."

Just like a machine, he thought.

After two easy Seminole outs, Scoot Robertson woke up the fans with a home run over the center field fence. The Seminoles went up on the scoreboard: 1–0.

Travis kept things alive with a clean hit between short and third. It got him to first base.

But Albie Carbone just couldn't get a piece of the ball. He struck out, and the Seminoles took to the field.

The Swordtails began to pick up steam at the plate in the next few innings. There was no rest now for the Seminoles out on the field. It took real concentration to hold the base runners from scoring.

Meanwhile, the Seminole hitting declined. Travis got to bat twice. Each time there were runners on base who had got there from walks. But he failed to drive them home. He went down twice on a series of strikes.

The Swordtail fans in the stands started to razz him, but he kept his cool. The machine was simply grinding away.

By the top of the fifth, the score was still 1–0.

As the Seminoles started for the field, Steffi pulled Travis aside.

"Don't worry about your hitting, Travis. That'll come back," she said. "You just don't want to make any mistakes out there. And keep your mind on the game and out of the movie theater! Remember what's at stake."

He didn't even blink at her. He just trotted out to his position. But he was jumpy inside. Why did she have to remind him? Didn't he have enough pressure on him, between the game and getting his video ready for the contest?

He managed to get his nerves under control so that he was ready for the first hit that came his way. He scooped it up and pegged it to Seth for the first out.

The next Swordtail at bat was Karim Kadar. Travis backed up to play him deep, just the way the coach wanted. No forgetting his advice this time.

Sure enough, Kadar popped one in his direction. But it was short. Travis had to make tracks to catch it in the air. He flung himself forward and hit the infield track on his stomach, but managed to get his glove under the ball in time.

Out number two.

The crowd cheered, and Travis was proud of himself for a moment. At least some people noticed that he was a person.

8

No amount of good Seminole fielding could have prevented the next change in the score. Paul walked Ron Marino, and Terry Wright came up to bat with two away.

Terry connected with the very first pitch. He belted the ball high and deep toward the left field fence — and over, for a home run. The scoreboard now read: Swordtails 2, Seminoles 1. Jake Santos flied out to end the Swordtails' turn at bat.

Travis was the leadoff batter for the Seminoles. He hadn't had any luck at bat since his single in the first inning. This time, after four straight balls, he found himself on first base at the bottom of the fifth.

And then Albie Carbone came out of his slump. He hit the ball so deep into right center field, he drove Travis home and landed on second base himself.

Chan Lee followed with a clean single that

advanced Albie to third. Then Peter came up to the plate.

Peter had been hitting deep into the outfield all day. The Swordtails backed up, looking for the long ball. But Peter surprised them. He pulled off a bunt that brought Albie home and took him safely to first. The score now read Seminoles 3, Swordtails 2.

With runners on first and third, Mert Farish came to the plate.

Mert's batting had been as strong as his fielding. He'd wound up on base well over half the times he'd come up to hit. But his streak finally ended. Bobby Meltzer put him down on two fouls and a called strike to end the inning.

"Three in a row!" called Steffi as the Seminoles moved out to the field.

"Heads-up ball, you guys!" shouted Dutch McLane.

What a difference from the last game, Travis thought. I don't feel tired, and this is the last inning. I guess that's what playing like a machine does. I'm ready for whatever comes my way.

It seemed as though the Swordtails had figured

that out. They did their best to keep the ball away from him. First Shelly Ross banged out a single down the first base line. He was followed at bat by Bobby Meltzer, who went down swinging.

Stan Weinberg, usually a strong hitter, had been having an off day at the plate. But he seemed ready to make up for it now.

Paul, who had relieved Georgie on the mound, stared him down, wound up, and threw the ball.

Strike one.

The next pitch was high and outside. One and one.

But the next pitch was just a little outside. It was a tough call. Stan stepped into it and swung.

Crack!

A line drive sizzled straight toward the shortstop position. It was high and looked as though it would zoom past Travis about two feet above his head.

He leaped for it at just the right moment and caught the ball in midair.

Shelly Ross had made a run for it. He had rounded second, and it was too late for him to go back. Travis slammed the ball to Scoot at third, who tagged Shelly for the final out.

The crowd went wild.

The Seminoles' fans rushed onto the field and hugged the players in the white-and-blue uniforms.

Scoot broke through the crowd and slapped a high five on Travis, followed by Chan and Seth. Paul worked his way over to give Travis a bear hug.

"Looks like you're a shoo-in for MVP, Travis," he said.

"Whoa! Don't jinx us," said Peter. "Let's keep our cool."

"We can win, win, win!" Howie Lander started to chant. Everyone picked it up. It echoed all over the field.

Then gradually the team paired off as usual and headed to their individual celebrations. They had been real friendly to Travis right after he saved the game. Now they seemed to forget him. Even Steffi had rushed off to join some of her girl-friends.

But Peter managed to pull himself away. He called over to Travis in the deserted dugout.

"Want some company?"

"Aren't you going off to celebrate with Seth or some of the guys?" Travis asked.

"Nah, they're just going to talk about the game and replay it over and over."

"Yeah, so?"

"I'd rather relax and get ready for the next one," Peter explained as they strolled down the street. "Hey, I have an idea. After dinner, why don't I come over so you can show me how you put together those videos? I don't know how you go about doing it."

"Sure, if you really want to," said Travis.

"'Course I do," said Peter. "I'll get there as soon as I can."

He turned off toward his own street and waved good-bye.

Travis forgot that he was supposed to be acting like a machine and jogged happily along the sidewalk until he reached home.

* * *

"Dad! Anybody home?" Travis called out.

"I'm up in the attic," came a voice from above.

"What's doing up there?" Travis called back. He trotted up the stairs and stood at the bottom of the pull-down ladder.

Mr. Bonelli's voice came back down, "I'm looking for some stuff we never unpacked."

"Like what?" asked Travis.

"My lucky shoes," said Mr. Bonelli.

"Didn't Mom throw those out?"

"I sure hope she didn't. No, here they are!" Mr. Bonelli exclaimed. "Way to go!"

Travis could hear him clumping around and slamming boxes shut. A few minutes later, Mr. Bonelli climbed down the ladder and waved a couple of scuffed bowling shoes in front of his son.

"Now there's a pair of winning shoes!" he said proudly.

Travis helped him put away the ladder and close off the attic.

"Do you really believe in things like lucky shoes, Dad?" he asked.

"Well, you don't want to take a chance with

67

these things," said Mr. Bonelli with a grin. "I'm usually not all that superstitious, but, well, I haven't been doing so well lately. Maybe these shoes will make a difference."

"Gee, Dad, maybe you haven't been getting enough rest," said Travis with a big smile on his face.

"Wise guy," Mr. Bonelli said, smiling back at him.

"Seriously, Dad," Travis said as they came downstairs. "What's so important about winning? About having the highest bowling average? About making the most hits? Why does everybody make such a big deal out of it, anyhow?"

"It's not that big a deal, Travis," said his father. "Everyone just wants to do his best, not to let the team down."

"The team! How much does your team care about you, Dad?" asked Travis. "Aren't they more interested in the number of pins you knock down?"

"What's going on, Travis?" asked Mr. Bonelli. "Of course the score counts. That's why we practice so much. But we're all pals, too, and when we're in a tournament, it's like we're all parts of one big machine, going for the win."

"That's just it — winning is supposed to be fun," said Travis. "Sometimes I wonder if . . . if —"

"Travis, you worry too much," said Mr. Bonelli. "Listen, here's what I think. I think that I don't feel like eating the rest of that roast chicken we had last night. We can have it tomorrow. Tell you what. I'm going down to the alley to see if these shoes still have the old magic in them. Just a few strings. And then I'll come back with a pizza for the two of us."

"Pepperoni and extra cheese?"

"Okay."

"And no anchovies."

"No anchovies."

"Great!" said Travis. "I'll set the table. And maybe I'll do some work on my videos while you're gone."

"Just don't forget to shut the light off there when you leave," said Mr. Bonelli. "Save electricity."

"Right, Dad," Travis said.

After his father left, he carefully arranged the plates, forks, knives, and extra napkins on the table. Then he went up to his workshop.

As usual, it was all neat and clean. Travis found the tape that had the scene he wanted. He popped it into the VCR on his left and turned on the unit in the middle, the editing controller. Then he got his master tape of his contest entry and popped it into the VCR on his right. He played the VCR on the left until the scene came on. Then he stopped it. He played the blank tape until he found the right spot for the new scene. He made the transfer, played it back, then rewound both tapes to their beginnings.

That done, Travis decided to call it quits for that day. As he was putting all the tapes away, he thought he heard the back door of the garage slam shut.

I'll bet that's Dad with the pizza, he thought. Funny, I didn't hear him drive up.

His stomach growled, and he hurried to finish cleaning up. As he rattled down the steps, he realized he had forgotten to turn off the light in

his workshop. He turned around to head back up when he noticed the garage was empty.

I'm sure I heard a door, he thought, mystified. But if it wasn't Dad, who was it?

Travis opened the back door and was about to leave the garage when he spied a small white envelope with his name printed on it in bold letters. He carried it with him to the kitchen and opened it up. Inside the envelope was a single piece of paper with two sentences written on it.

"Get your act together. You'd better score at least two runs in the next game — or else!" Beside this warning someone had drawn a scowling face.

Travis turned the paper over and then examined the envelope. There were no other marks besides the words and the face picture.

It has to be the same wise guy who's been calling, he thought darkly. I'm sure it's some weirdo. Some crank. Some crazy Seminole fan, maybe.

But who?

Mr. Bonelli arrived with the pizza a few minutes later.

"Travis, you don't get one bite until you go and shut off that light in the garage, I could see it from three streets over," he said.

Travis didn't bother to explain that he'd forgotten it when he found the note. Why bother his father about some silly crackpot?

When he finally got to the pizza, he noticed a big grin on his father's face.

"Let me guess," said Travis. "The lucky shoes?"

"Two strikes in a row," said Mr. Bonelli.

Maybe I'd better find some lucky shoes, thought Travis, to shut up that crazy fan.

But the next day at batting practice, wearing his regular cleats, his hitting was in great form. In fact, Paul Farley even complained, "Can't get anything by you today, Travis. Hope I do better with the Swordtails."

This put Travis in a pretty good mood. He was a lot more relaxed than usual when he got home later that day. As he opened the back door, he knew immediately that his mother was there. He saw bags of groceries on the table, damp clothes in the laundry basket, the water running in the sink, and heard the sound of Mrs. Bonelli's voice talking on the telephone.

"So you'll try to deliver those curtains by noon tomorrow?" she was saying in her sweetest voice. After she hung up, she groaned, "Fat chance. Well, maybe we'll get them before the end of the week. Travis! You're home!"

She gave him a big hug, freed one arm, and slipped a glass vase under the running faucet.

"There are some flowers in a bucket out back — would you bring them in? We're not going out for dinner — I can't wait to make this wonderful chowder I had out West," the words all flew out in one long string as she bustled about.

"I'm glad you're home, Mom," he said when he returned with the flowers. But Mrs. Bonelli was back on the phone.

"You do have fresh spinach? Good, I'll send someone right over."

She hung up.

"Travis, I want to hear about everything I've missed while I was gone. How are you doing with your baseball team? Dad told me you may go to the World Series if the Semaphores win."

"*Seminoles*, Mom!"

"Right, just tell me what's going on."

"The play-off series is tied right now," he said.

"Good, you still have a chance. That's wonderful. Now what was I doing? Oh, yes, spinach. I'm glad they have fresh spinach. That will help build you up for the play-offs."

"Mom, I'm not Popeye the Sailor," Travis groaned.

She hugged him again, reached behind him, and poured out a glass of milk.

"No, you're not, but I love spinach salad," she admitted. "Plus I'm tired of eating off a little tray with tiny compartments. So, would you mind going to the market for me and picking it up? It's all ordered."

"Okay, you win — I'll go for the spinach," he said.

He walked out the kitchen door and saw Steffi standing in his driveway. She was tossing a whiffle ball up and down, from one hand to another.

"Want to hit a few?" she asked.

"Can't," he said. "I have to do an errand."

"Where?"

"The market. I have to pick something up for my mother," he said.

"Okay, I'll go with you," she announced.

"Glad I invited you," he said in a mock sarcastic voice.

When they got there, he pulled a shopping cart from the parking lot.

"I thought you only had to get one thing," said Steffi.

Travis shook his head. "You don't know my mother. She'll have thought of a dozen more by now. Watch."

He went inside and spoke to the store manager. "Hi, I'm Travis Bonelli. Has my mother called?"

The store manager nodded and handed him a list.

"See?" he said to Steffi. "That's my Mom, for you. My Dad is super-organized, but my mother has a million things going all at once."

"Okay, so what's on the list?" she asked.

They pushed the cart down an aisle filled with potato chips, popcorn, candy, and all kinds of snacks.

"We'd better get away from this stuff fast.

Before we get into trouble," said Travis, hurrying down the aisle. As he worked the cart around a pyramid of breakfast cereal boxes, he felt someone nudge him from behind.

It was Mert Farish!

"Now, don't go bananas — whoops, I mean bonkers, Travis," said the Seminoles' catcher. "That didn't hurt and you know it. I was just fooling around."

Steffi rushed down the aisle.

"Are you two guys at it again?" she asked.

"No, Mert couldn't resist blindsiding me," said Travis, trying to be a good sport. "No harm done this time."

"Good, then I can go and find the ginger ale," she said.

"Aisle five," said Mert.

When Steffi was gone, Mert said to Travis, "Glad you've lightened up a little. So you can take a joke after all."

Mert's words made Travis suddenly suspicious. He decided to play his hunch.

"You think it's a *joke* making those dumb phone

calls?" said Travis. "Telling me I had to start hitting . . . or else?"

Mert's eyes widened. "What are you talking about?" he asked. "*I* got a phone call like that the other day. Those were the exact words. And I thought it might be *you!*"

"Oh, sure," said Travis. "Great story, Mert, but why should I believe you?"

"Why should I believe you!" snapped Mert. He stormed off.

Steffi came back with the ginger ale and dropped it into the cart.

"Good to see you two guys getting along," she said sarcastically. "C'mon, let's finish up this shopping."

They quickly gathered the rest of the items from the list and headed to the checkout line. After they had paid for the groceries, Steffi bought a piece of bubble gum. She tore it open carefully, pulled out a slip of paper, and studied it.

"My fortune," she informed Travis, showing him the paper.

"You are destined for great things," it read.

There was a thumbs-up sign after the sentence.

"I thought fortunes only came in cookies," said Travis. He handed the paper back to her.

Steffi popped the gum in her mouth and shoved the fortune in her pocket. "Cookies, bubble gum, whatever. At least this time I got a good one. I hate when I get the gloom-and-doom ones," she said with a grin. "Sure hope it's talking about the World Series. That'd be great enough for me!"

Travis groaned as he picked up the bags of groceries. "It'd be great enough for me if you carried one of these. This ginger ale is heavy!"

9

During the warm-up for the third game in the play-off series, Travis looked over to the bench. Steffi was writing down the roster in her scorecard. She had no time for him or for anyone else.

Like a machine, he thought. Good, I'll be just like a machine, too. I'll go on automatic pilot. After all, that's what the guys seem to expect of me. Play, play, play — don't think.

The Swordtails ran out to the field as the Seminoles led off. There was a new player in gray with red trim on the mound. Both teams were starting off with new pitchers. Southpaw Lou Lanahan now faced the top of the Seminole lineup.

Seth Franklin was at the plate.

"Show 'im your stuff, Seth," called Howie from the on-deck circle.

But Seth was just the first of the Seminole batters to have trouble with a left-handed pitcher. He went down swinging for the first out.

It was the same story with the next two Seminoles. Howie woofed three straight pitches. Scoot managed to get off a few foul balls before he struck out.

Georgie Greene, the Seminoles' new pitcher, didn't do as well. His right-handed delivery was a little faster than Paul Farley's, but he wasn't as accurate. The Swordtails zeroed in on his weaknesses right off.

Their shortstop, Stan Weinberg, led off with a clean single just over Howie's head. Then Zang Blakewell belted one just short of Peter Hooper's reach in left field.

But with two men on, Georgie settled down and held off the next two hitters with strikeouts.

Swordtail third baseman Ron Marino came up to bat with runners still on first and second. They were looking for someone to drive them home.

Georgie's first two pitches were high and outside.

With a 2-and-0 count, he rocketed one down the middle that caught Marino unaware. The count went to 2 and 1.

A swing and a miss produced strike number two.

And then a ball so low that it almost raised the dust at the plate brought the count to 3 and 2.

The crowd was silent, waiting for the next pitch.

Travis didn't seem very concerned. His mind was elsewhere. He shuffled around in his position, making moves automatically. But he was thinking about getting his application form in. After he read the rules, he realized he didn't have to send the video along with it. But because the contest only took a limited number of applicants, he had to send in his form and deposit right away. He'd ask his mom to get him a money order at the bank to send along with the application.

With his mind a million miles away, he was caught short when a ground ball was hit in his direction. Because he was lost in thought, he got a bad jump on it.

Howie, luckily, raced over and managed to snag the ball in the webbing of his glove. Then, on his knees, he whirled and fired it home. Mert caught the ball and tagged the runner just inches away from the plate.

The Seminoles' fans exploded. It was Howie's biggest play of the series. They rewarded him with thunderous applause when the Seminoles came off the field.

In all the commotion, nobody mentioned that it really should have been Travis's play. If Howie hadn't gotten the ball, the shortstop could have been charged with an error. It was a lucky break for Travis.

He would have thanked Howie if he'd had the chance. But the Seminole shortstop was the lead-off batter.

Maybe I'll get one of the home runs that mystery caller wanted, he thought as he toed up to the plate.

This was his first encounter with the left-handed hurler. He did no better than the three Seminoles before him. He swung at — and missed — the first two pitches. He was called out on the third.

Passing by the next batter, Albie Carbone, he just shrugged.

"Take your time with this guy, Travis," said Coach McLane. "Next time don't be in such a hurry. He'll make his mistakes. You have to watch for them."

As usual, Travis didn't say anything. He just flopped down at the opposite end of the bench from Steffi and stared out at the field. He wasn't interested in talking to anyone.

From the corner of his eye, he noticed Peter slide over next to the scorekeeper.

Every now and then they glanced over at him.

They're probably talking about me, he thought. Probably analyzing why I didn't get a hit. Maybe they're feeding information to the mystery caller.

Meanwhile, at the plate, Albie looked as though he was going to be the first Seminole to get by the new pitcher. He hit the ball deep into left field for an easy single. But he tried to stretch it and was tagged out at second base.

With two away, the Seminoles looked like they were going down one-two-three. Chan Lee, their next hitter, was their only chance to do something about that.

He did. After a called strike, he pounded the

next pitch. It went all the way for his first home run of the play-offs. It put the Seminoles on the scoreboard: 1–0.

The bench cleared as the team rushed out to home plate to congratulate Chan. Travis trotted out with the rest of the guys.

The celebration was short lived. Peter was the next batter. He stood there as Lanahan pitched three balls in a row, followed by three strikes.

"Okay, you guys," called Steffi. "Let's hold on to that lead."

She talks just like one of the players, thought Travis, settling in at short. Maybe that's why she gets along with everyone, like Mert, and like Peter. Maybe they're all in on those phone calls. It could have been Peter on the phone the other day. I wouldn't know his voice if he disguised it. Yeah, maybe that was it . . . and he was just talking to Steffi about it.

He tried to figure out what Peter's voice would sound like with a handkerchief around the phone, or maybe a towel. Maybe he could ask Mert what the voice sounded like to him — *if* Mert was telling the truth about getting a call, too.

Travis was so lost in his thoughts, again, he hardly noticed that Jake Santos had made it to first. But then Shelly Ross belted a line drive straight at him. This time he stuck out his glove automatically and snagged the ball in the air — then flipped it to Georgie on the mound.

Jake had taken off from first after the pitch, but spun back when Travis caught the ball. He was still steps away from the bag.

A groan from the crowd was the first clue Travis had that he'd messed up. Scoot and Howie came running over to him.

"Travis, what's with you? That was the easiest pickoff anyone could have asked for!" hissed Scoot in a blistering whisper.

"Yeah, Trav, are you missing a few marbles or what?" asked Howie.

Travis just shook his head and stared at the ground.

Howie started to give him a friendly tap on the shoulder but stopped short.

As the two basemen returned to their positions, Travis could hear Scoot mutter, "Ice cube!"

But underneath his stony face, Travis was red hot with anger at himself for messing up.

Over at second, Jake gave Travis a big smile.

The whole Swordtail team was happy at the end of the inning. After fanning their pitcher, Georgie delivered a meatball to Stan Weinberg, who easily put it over the left field fence.

The score now read: Swordtails 2, Seminoles 1.

When the Seminoles finally came off the field, Coach McLane called Travis to one side.

"Travis, I don't know what's going on out there. Are you sick or something?"

"No, I'm okay," Travis mumbled. "Just a little slow warming up."

"Well, shake a leg, or do something to get that circulation going," said the coach. "I can't have someone whose brain is on half power out there."

Georgie managed to keep the Swordtails from scoring during the next few innings. Travis didn't have much to do at his position. Even though his mind bounced around between the game and the video contest and the mystery caller, he managed not to mess up.

He came up to bat again in the fifth inning. The Seminoles were still down by one run. There were runners on first and third with one out.

Travis left the on-deck circle and stepped up to the plate. He gazed out at the field, then briefly glanced toward the stands. Was the mystery caller sitting up there, waiting for him to hit a homer?

Oh, well, might as well try to get a hit, at least, Travis thought.

He let the first pitch go by for a called strike, then swung at the next. It popped up foul toward the third base line. Shelly Ross caught it easily, then pegged it to Ron Marino at third, who picked off the runner for a double play.

When Travis returned to the dugout to pick up his glove, Coach McLane shook his head.

"Take a seat, Travis. I'm putting Jimmy in."

Jimmy Melville had been the regular shortstop before Travis. He'd hit a slump in his batting, and the coach had given the newcomer a chance at the job midway through the season. Travis had made the position his own, and Jimmy had been a utility player ever since.

Travis could see Steffi entering Jimmy's name on the scorecard. He slumped down on the almost-empty bench.

She slid over to him and whispered, "Didn't you see his signal?"

"What signal?" he asked, surprised.

"The signal to bunt!" she said. "It was plain as could be."

"I guess I missed it," mumbled Travis. "That's all."

"That's all?" said Steffi. "It could have cost us the game, that's all!"

She went back to her scorekeeping. Travis smoldered quietly on the bench.

The Swordtails managed to hold on to their lead and add to it.

In the bottom of the fifth inning, they put three men on base and brought them home one by one. Georgie Greene just couldn't seem to get the ball by them.

In the last inning, with two outs, Mert Farish put one over the center field fence for a home run. It helped to keep the Seminoles alive.

Maybe that will make him happy, so he'll get

off my case, thought Travis. He still wasn't con-vinced that Mert hadn't made the mystery phone calls.

But Mert's homer wasn't enough to launch a rally. The game ended with the score Swordtails 5, Seminoles 2.

In the play-off series, the Seminoles were now down by one game.

10

An air of gloom hung over the team as the coach gathered them together in the dugout. He did his best to rally their spirits, but as they left the field, they still had a long way to go.

This time, Travis didn't linger. He rushed off as soon as the team meeting broke up.

On the way home, he was really miserable. This was the first time he'd ever been taken out of a game.

What went wrong? He'd tried to play just like a machine, but maybe that wasn't enough. He didn't get all the moves right automatically. But even worse, he'd let his mind wander. There were just too many things going on at once. So the truth was he really hadn't played his best, and the coach did the right thing.

He was glad his folks hadn't been at the game. But they'd want to know how it went. And of course he would tell them what happened. He knew they would be sorry for him but would try to give him some kind of boost.

Maybe he could simply say that the Seminoles lost and leave it at that. After all, Dad would probably be wound up in his bowling team. And Mom would probably be wound up just being wound up.

Maybe he was just feeling the pressure from the mystery caller. Plus he really needed to put some effort into getting his video ready. And to tell the truth, he liked spending time with Steffi. That movie had been fun — until Mert showed up. And of course he had fun watching videos with Peter. It wasn't easy keeping track of all the people and all the things going on.

Thinking about all these things, Travis almost walked by his own house. Instead, he marched into the kitchen and opened the refrigerator. He poured himself a large glass of milk and reached into the cookie jar. Good, peanut butter cookies, his favorite. It was great having Mom home. She was tops in the baking department — even Dad agreed.

The cookies gave him just enough of a lift to get

him to his workshop. He took out the contest application and looked it over carefully. There were just a few blanks left to fill in. In crisp, block letters, he printed the missing information. Then he carefully folded the application and put it into the envelope. He didn't lick it and seal it because he still needed the check.

After that, he ran through the rough version of the video as far as he had gotten with it. As always, there were parts he loved and parts he thought were hokey. Maybe a combination of those two kinds of scenes would turn out right.

But as he worked on the video, his mind drifted back to the game. He still felt miserable about being pulled. If only there were someone he could talk to about it. Steffi had a one-track mind, and Peter was completely focused on winning the series. No one else on the team seemed to know he was alive after a game was over.

Thinking about the game reminded him that his folks would be rolling in for dinner soon. He hadn't heard the car pull up, so he decided he had time to surprise them.

Travis pulled out all the stops. He set the table

in the dining room with all the nice dishes and glasses. He even found a vase and filled it with cut flowers for the center of the table.

He thought about going upstairs to clean his room.

No, that would be too much, he realized. They'd be sure to know something was wrong if he did that without being reminded.

It was almost dinnertime, but still no sign of his folks.

Brinnnng! Brinnnnng!

If that was the mystery caller . . .

Travis carefully picked up the phone.

"Hello?" he said very cautiously.

"Travis, it's Peter," said the voice at the other end of the line.

"Oh, Peter, I thought it might be . . . uh . . . my folks."

"Nah, it's just me," said Peter. "Hey, listen, I'm sorry about the game today."

"Yeah, me, too," said Travis.

"I mean, I wouldn't get too shook up about it," said Peter. "Coach McLane knows what a terrific player you are. You'll be back in the lineup in no time."

"Thanks," said Travis.

"And I hope you're not mad at me or something," said Peter. "I mean, I get real serious when we're playing, and I don't pay much attention to anything else."

"No big deal," said Travis.

"Good! So you want to watch some videos later?" Peter asked. "Got anything new you want me to see?"

"Yeah, as a matter of fact," said Travis. "There's something really special I want to show you. Why don't you come right over after dinner?"

"Great," said Peter. "Tell you what. I'll pick up some frozen yogurt to have while we watch."

"Terrific," said Travis. "See you later, Peter."

He hung up the phone. The call made him feel better. It gave him a little more courage for telling his parents about the game.

He heard the sound of a car grinding up the driveway. Someone was home.

"Travis? Are you there?" Mrs. Bonelli called

out. "Can you give me a hand with these bundles?"

"Sure," he said. He jogged out the back door to the driveway. "Where's Dad? How come he's not home yet? Are we going to have dinner soon? I'm kind of hungry."

"Your father had to work late," said Mrs. Bonelli. "He's going straight to the bowling alley. He'll grab something there. But I picked up a special treat for us — fresh swordfish. I thought we'd grill it and have a picnic out back."

Swordfish! It reminded him of the Sword-tails — and the game that afternoon.

His mother went inside the house. She saw the dining room and cried, "Travis! What a nice surprise. We'll just cook the swordfish outside and eat it in here. Just the two of us."

During dinner, Travis tried to stall the inevitable. He asked Mrs. Bonelli about her last trip. She always had a bunch of interesting stories to tell about the passengers or sometimes the crew. They had almost gotten as far as dessert when she brought up the play-offs.

"I can't believe I haven't heard anything about

the game today, Travis," she said. "What happened? Did your team win?"

Travis carefully wiped his mouth with his napkin — and then poured out the whole story of what had happened. He told her about having so many things on his mind at once, like the video contest and the play-offs at the same time.

"So I thought I could just turn on the old machine and play the game without thinking about it," he explained. "And I blew it."

"It's okay to make mistakes, Travis," Mrs. Bonelli said.

"I know, as long as you do your best, right?"

"Right." She nodded. "And as long as you have the right attitude."

"I guess so," he mumbled. He wasn't sure what the right attitude was.

"Travis, it's no use playing if you don't enjoy it and the people you're playing with," she said. "How can you do your best if you're not enjoying the challenge?"

"But I love playing baseball," he said.

"That's fine," she said. "But you have to put your whole heart into it while you're playing.

Your coach and teammates will notice if you don't. And you can't kill yourself trying to do something else at the same time."

Travis played with a piece of squeezed-out lemon on his plate.

"I'm going to make myself some tea," she said. "Let me see what there is for dessert."

"No, thanks," Travis said. "Peter's coming over with some frozen yogurt. We're going to look at some videos in my workshop."

She went out to put the kettle on.

Travis sat there thinking about what she had said. He remembered overhearing Scoot call him an ice cube. Maybe his teammates didn't want a machine after all.

Travis stood up, plate in hand, his mind whirling. Maybe he was trying to do too many things at once — when he didn't have to. And he was trying to be perfect at them all at the same time. The perfect shortstop. The perfect video maker.

But the play-offs were right now. And the video didn't have to be in for ninety days!

Boy, what a dummy he was. He could send in

the application and worry about the video *after* the *Seminoles* won the series.

He went into the kitchen. His mother was sitting and waiting for the kettle to boil. He leaned over and kissed her on her cheek. Then, without a word, he headed for his workshop.

I'll clean things up, grab an oldie to show Peter, and then shut down operations in the workshop until after the series, he said to himself as he climbed the stairs.

The minute he crossed the threshold, he knew something was wrong. Someone else might not have noticed, but Travis could tell at a glance that things weren't where they should have been.

Someone's been messing around in here, he thought. But *messing* wasn't really the right word. It was still pretty neat. Nothing was broken or tossed on the floor.

He went over to the worktable. The contest application he had just finished filling out was no longer there.

He looked all around. The contest guidelines were still there, but there was no doubt that the application was gone. And during his search, he discovered something else. At least a half-dozen of his videos were gone. The missing tapes included *Travis's Tales of Terror, Part One, Part Two,* and *Part Three,* as well as the werewolf movie and the oldie about the lady and the telephone.

But, worst of all, there was one more tape missing, the one labeled *W.I.P.*

11

Travis thought it might be Peter playing a practical joke. He carefully crept out of the workshop and tiptoed all around the garage, inside and out.

No sign of Peter anywhere.

He decided to call the Hooper house to see if Peter was still there, or when he'd left.

But as he walked out of the garage door, he could hear Peter whistling down the street. He was carrying the bag with the frozen yogurt.

"Hi, Trav," said Peter, all smiles. "Here's the goodies. My dad dropped me off on his way to the bowling alley. Maybe we ought to put this in the freezer till we're ready to have it."

Peter handed him the frozen yogurt. It was hard as a brick.

Well, that pretty much takes care of where Peter was, Travis thought.

"Come on up," he said. "I have some bad news."

After Travis pointed out what had happened, Peter scratched his head.

"I don't get it," he said. "Why would anyone want to take your videotapes, anyhow? You and I are the only ones I know who really like horror movies. And what's the point of stealing your contest application? You can go and get another, can't you?"

"I suppose so," said Travis. He picked up the guidelines and quickly scanned them. "The application and entry fee aren't due for another few weeks. And I've still got the original movies to work with, so I can always piece *W.I.P.* back together." Travis sighed. "But you know what, Peter? My heart just isn't in it right now. I think maybe I ought to concentrate on the play-offs and that's it."

"Trav, I couldn't agree more," said Peter. "But I'm sorry it had to happen this way. Tell you what, after the play-offs, I'll help you. I mean, I can't do anything about putting together the tape, but I'll sit and watch all the oldies you want to find good scenes for a new one, okay?"

Travis smiled. "Sure," he said. "I still can't believe someone took them."

"Maybe you have a secret fan," Peter suggested. "You know, somebody like . . . like old lady McGonnagle."

"Her? The music teacher? You've got to be kidding!"

"No, I'm not, Travis, honest," said Peter. He tried to hide the smirk on his face. "Remember when you first came into the class, how she said, 'Oh, Travis, you have such a lovely tenor voice! You should sing a solo in our glee club!'"

"I wanted to crawl into the cracks in the floor," said Travis. "That's why I rushed off to try out for the baseball team. The glee club rehearsed after school the same time as spring practice."

"Baloney," said Peter. "You tried out for the team 'cause you're a natural. You have the best swing at bat, and you're a terrific shortstop."

"So, if I'm so terrific, why'd I get pulled from the game?" said Travis.

"Come on, Trav," said Peter. "Even the pros have bad days."

"All right, all right," said Travis. It's just . . . it's just . . ."

"Just what?" asked Peter. He settled down into the leather chair.

"Never mind."

"C'mon, Travis, tell me what's bugging you," said Peter. "I'm your pal, right? That's what pals are for."

"I guess you're right. Okay. See, I love playing baseball, I mean, really love the game. It's just that with the Seminoles, I never feel like I'm part of the team."

"Trav, it's a two-way street," said Peter.

"What do you mean?"

"You don't give, you don't get," Peter explained. "The guys think you're a real glacier. Oh, you hit and field like all get-out, but you never really show how you feel about anything."

"I'm a lot like you there, Peter," said Travis. "I'm usually just concentrating on doing my best."

Of course, thought Travis, sometimes my mind's a million miles away. But that's going to change from now on.

"You know," said Travis. "Maybe it's a good thing I don't have the video contest to worry about right now. Maybe the tapes will turn up later — like after we've won the play-offs."

There was a day off before the next game in the play-off series. Coach McLane used it for a practice to keep his players warmed up.

After he ran a few drills, he called the whole team together.

"Today," he announced, "we're going to do something different. Nobody's going to play his regular position. You're all going to swap. I want you guys to see what it's like from another angle for a change. Then maybe you'll pay better attention to teamwork."

He held out his cap. Inside it were folded-up pieces of paper with two sets of positions written on them. Some were in blue ink, the others in red.

"If you get your own position, toss it back in and take another," he said.

Peter was the first to pick.

"First base on the blue team. Way to go!" he said. "A nice short trip to work."

Seth unfolded his slip of paper. "Oh, no! Pitcher for the red! I'll wear my arm out."

"Take it easy," said the coach. "I don't want you playing full barrel. Let's go real slow. There aren't any scouts from the major leagues watching."

Mert Farish looked at his pick, shrugged, and turned away silently.

"Look at this," said Howie, waving his draw over his head. "It says, 'Scorekeeper'!"

"Really?" asked Albie. "Red or blue?"

"Gotcha!" Howie laughed. "No, I'm out in left field for the reds."

Travis finally pulled a piece of paper from the cap. He opened it and shook his head.

"What did you get, Travis?" asked Peter.

Travis looked toward home plate. "Catcher, blue," he said.

"Figures," said Mert. "I got the blue team short position."

"Good," said the coach. "Everybody all set now? Let's get started."

Chan Lee was the blue team's pitcher. He threw a few warm-ups, nice and easy. Travis managed to catch them without any trouble.

Then the red team came up to bat. They had a lot of fun. They hit almost everything Chan threw. Travis laughed when he saw how much trouble Mert had at short.

Very few pitches crossed the plate. After a while it got a little boring, and Travis's mind wandered to the theft of his videos. He was surprised how little it bothered him. He had always saved everything and knew he could replace just about everything. And there was plenty of time after the play-offs were over.

Suddenly he felt a thud against his chest protector. Chan Lee had gained enough confidence to rocket in a fastball.

It went right by the batter, then bounced off the absent-minded catcher. It hit the dirt right in front of the plate.

Travis thought the batter might have tipped the ball, so he scooped it up and pegged it to Peter at first base.

That was all a red team runner on third needed. He crossed the plate standing up.

Coach McLane groaned.

Peter flipped the ball to Chan and shook his head. And out at shortstop, Mert Farish had a big smile on his face.

12

It was only a silly practice game, but Travis felt like a fool. He'd messed up once again because he hadn't been paying attention. Oh, sure, he could blame it on the new position. But he knew enough to watch out for a man on third.

For the rest of the practice, he kept his eyes and his mind on the game right in front of him. It was a good thing, too, because Coach McLane switched positions after a few innings. This time Travis ended up in right field. That was a hard place to stay awake sometimes in a regular game. But this time Scoot Robertson was the pitcher. The red team kept slugging the ball into the outfield. Travis had his work cut out for him.

Whenever he batted, he held his own. He walked once and then went 3 for 3, all solid hits.

By the time he got home, he was just as tired as if he'd played a full game.

"Your mother got a call," Mr. Bonelli said when

Travis walked into the kitchen. "Seems like half the crew has the flu, so she had to go and fill in."

"Aw, I was hoping she'd be home a little longer," said Travis.

"Well, the good news is she's going to have a full two-weeks off when she gets back. So we'll catch up on a bunch of things then, okay?" said his father. "We'll come out to see you play. Or maybe we'll go to some movies together. Or maybe we'll go out to eat at that fancy restaurant in town."

"What about your bowling?" Travis asked.

"The team's doing fine," said Mr. Bonelli. "I've met some great guys, and we have a lot of fun. But I think I was starting to get a little carried away. It's time to put first things first."

Travis thought long and hard on what his father was saying. The rattle of the dishes made him realize he was hungry.

"What's for dinner?" he asked.

"Tuna noodle casserole," said Mr. Bonelli. "Best I could do on short notice."

"Ice cream for dessert?" asked Travis.

"Just get cleaned up," said his father.

After dinner, when the dishes were all put away, Mr. Bonelli went into the living room. Travis followed.

"Want to see what's on TV, Dad?" he asked.

"You'll probably find one of your *Happy Horror* flicks," said Mr. Bonelli. "Go ahead, let's see how long I can last."

He took an open bag of potato chips from the kitchen and settled down on the living room couch.

Travis flipped from channel to channel. At last he found what he was looking for: *Revenge of the Quicksand Monster.*

On the TV screen, a strange creature crawled out of a slimy marsh. A strange voice screeched, "Revenge! Revenge!"

"This is going to be great, Dad," said Travis. "Wait till you see what happens next!"

Mr. Bonelli burrowed into the surrounding sofa cushions. Despite himself, he was glued to the television screen.

Brinnnng! Brinnnng!

"Stay where you are, Travis. I'll get it," said Mr.

Bonelli, springing to his feet. "It's probably some-one from my bowling team. Or your mother."

With one eye on the TV screen, Mr. Bonelli flipped a handful of potato chips into his mouth, then turned to pick up the phone in the hallway. He barely managed to choke out a crunched "Hello" into the receiver. He listened for a moment and then demanded angrily, "Who is this?" Travis looked up quickly.

"Hello! Hello!" Mr. Bonelli shouted into the phone.

Travis pressed the *mute* button on the remote control. "Was that Mom?" he asked.

"It certainly wasn't!" Ken Bonelli snapped. "I think it was some lunatic who thought he was talking to you!"

"To me?" asked Travis. "What . . . what did he say?"

"Something about playing heads-up ball — or else," replied his father. "Have any idea who it was?"

"Maybe," said Travis.

"Maybe?"

"Well, see, that wasn't the first call like that."

"Maybe you'd better shut off that TV and tell me what's going on."

Travis hit the *off* button on the remote just as the strange creature started sinking into the quicksand. Luckily he had seen this movie before. He knew what would happen in the end.

"Now, start at the beginning," said Mr. Bonelli.

Travis told him about the first call and how he didn't think anything of it. Then he told him about the missing videotapes.

"That's serious," said Mr. Bonelli. "Why, it's breaking and entering as well as theft."

"Nothing was broken, Dad," said Travis. "And the garage door is always open."

"That's true," said Mr. Bonelli.

"It really got to me at first," said Travis. "In fact, the phone calls were part of the reason I played so badly that the coach had to pull me from the game. But then I figured it's just like someone's shouting names at me, like from the stands. And remember 'sticks and stones'?"

"That's true, names won't hurt you," admitted Mr. Bonelli, calming down a little. "But is there

113

anyone you can think of who might want to scare you by stealing your tapes?"

"No," said Travis. But an idea formed in the back of his mind. "Except . . ."

"Except who?" asked his father.

"Well, Mert Farish has been acting kind of mean lately," he said.

"What do you mean?"

Travis told him about the incidents in front of Peter's house and in the market.

"That's interesting," said Mr. Bonelli. "The Farish boy's father is on my bowling team, too."

"You never mentioned that," said Travis.

"You never mentioned Mert before. Anyhow, I gather that he used to be real pals with the Hooper boy," said Mr. Bonelli. "But now Mert thinks Peter's deserted him, that he's suddenly become a video freak."

"Like me," said Travis. "Maybe that's why Mert's been making those calls. And maybe he took the videos."

"Maybe I ought to talk with him, or his father," said Mr. Bonelli.

"Please, Dad, don't," said Travis. "If it isn't

114

Mert, I'll look like a big baby. That would be worse. I can find out by myself."

"Don't go playing Dick Tracy, Travis," warned Mr. Bonelli.

"I'll be cool, Dad. Don't worry," said Travis. "I'll just keep an eye out during the game tomorrow."

"Fine, but keep your mind on the game. You never know when the coach might put you back in," said his father. "In fact, your first job is to be there for the team. You can talk to Mert after the game."

"That's exactly what I'll do," Travis promised.

"Good," said Mr. Bonelli. "In the meantime, I'm going to put a lock on the garage door, just in case. And I'm going to try to get away from work a little early. I haven't seen one of your play-off games yet. Have to support the team, you know."

"Wish I could be sure you'll see me play," said Travis. "Now I'm getting really psyched up for the game."

"Maybe you'd better cool down. Let's finish watching that quicksand movie."

"It's all over now," said Travis. "That was the ending we saw just before the phone rang."

"Some ending," said his father. "Tell you what, then. I challenge you to a game of Scrabble. Think you're good enough to beat your old man?"

Travis nodded. "Uh-huh."

He got out the Scrabble box and turned over the letters. They each drew one. Travis picked the letter *D*. His father turned over a *W*.

"You go first," said Mr. Bonelli.

Travis picked six more letters and placed them on the stand in front of him. He had a *G*, an *E*, an *A*, an *N*, an *R*, and an *X*, to go along with his *D*. What could he do with *G*, *E*, *A*, *N*, *R*, *X*, and *D?*

"Can you make something out of your letters?" his father asked.

Travis paused for a moment. Then it came to him.

"I can use six of them," he said.

Starting with the pink square in the middle, he laid out his word: *DANGER*.

There was one letter left over, the *X*.

X marks the spot, he thought, staring at the letter.

It looked as though the letter were staring right back at him.

13

Was he imagining it — or was Mert dodging him?

Travis arrived at the field a little early for the game. Even though he'd said he wasn't going to ask Mert anything until after the game, he might find out something just by keeping his eyes and ears open. Mert might just mention where he was the night before when the mystery caller had struck.

But the Seminoles' catcher managed to avoid him.

Just as well, thought Travis. Better pay attention to the game, even though I'm not sure I'll get off the bench.

Coach McLane didn't say much to him during the warm-up. But when it came time for the game to start, he signaled Jimmy Melville to take the shortstop slot.

Travis was disappointed. He really wanted to

help the Seminoles, and it was hard being left on the bench. But he knew it wouldn't help if he grumbled or complained. Instead, he was determined to follow the action, to be ready to go if the coach called on him.

Paul Farley was on the mound for the Seminoles. He struck out the first batter. Then he faced the Swordtail right fielder, Zang Blakewell. Zang was capable of hitting the long ball, so the Seminoles played him deep.

He fanned the first pitch. He connected with the second. It was a line drive just out of Scoot Robertson's reach. Zang reached first base easily but tried to stretch it to second. Scoot made a bad throw to Howie, so Zang pushed on toward third.

Jimmy tried to help cover the throw but got in the runner's way. There was a collision. Jimmy was knocked down — and Zang was safe at third.

Jimmy got up limping. He winced in pain as he tried to settle into the shortstop position. Dutch McLane called for a time out. Howie and Scoot helped Jimmy off the field.

The coach examined Jimmy's ankle with an experienced eye. "Looks like a sprain," he said.

"Let's get some ice on it. Travis, you'd better get out there."

Travis felt sorry for Jimmy and was glad the injury wasn't serious. He couldn't help feeling excited, though, about the chance to play. He was determined not to make any mistakes.

Paul managed to finish the inning without letting Zang make it home. He struck out the next batter. Then Mert saved him by catching a pop-up foul.

Leading off for the Seminoles, Seth got a clean single down the middle. But Howie and Scoot both went down swinging. Travis followed them at bat. He hit three foul balls in a row. Then he belted a line drive straight into the Swordtail second baseman's waiting glove for the third out.

The second inning went scoreless for both teams. But in the top of the third inning, the Swordtails managed to load the bases with only one out.

Karim Kadar came up to bat.

"Keep your eyes open!" shouted the Seminoles' coach to his infield.

It was good advice. Kadar swung at a fastball

and connected. The ball went rocketing between Travis and Scoot.

It looked like a fair hit, enough for the runners to advance. They all took off.

But Travis was on his toes and managed to snag it on one bounce. He pivoted and pegged it home for one out. Mert's throw to third was just a little too late for a double play. The bases remained loaded.

The next Swordtail batter, Ron Marino, hit a wobbler that Paul himself picked up for a quick toss home to retire the side.

There was plenty of action next when the Seminoles took to the plate. Chan got on base right away. Then Peter belted one that drove Chan to third after he squeaked into second by an eyelash.

Next at bat, Mert Farish cracked one that sailed out to the center field wall. It sent the two men on base all the way home. Mert tried to stretch his hit to third base but was tagged a little short of the bag for the out.

There was no more scoring that inning. But at least the Seminoles could look up at the scoreboard and see themselves ahead: 2–0.

Travis kept his wits about him on the field. In the next two innings, he made several terrific catches. There could be no complaints about the way he handled himself out on the field.

In the dugout, while he was waiting for his turn at bat, he allowed his mind to wander just a little bit. He couldn't completely forget about the weird phone calls and the stolen videotapes. But at least he didn't keep running scenes from horror videos on his mental tape player. That could all wait until after the series.

Or could it?

He had a glimmer of interest in the contest running through his thoughts as he came up to bat. Before he knew it, he was batting on automatic pilot.

"Strike three! You're out!"

Feeling miserable, Travis dropped his bat in the rack and flopped down at the end of the bench.

"Your average is for the birds, Travis," Steffi announced, chewing away at her gum. She blew a big pink bubble and let it burst. He stared down at his cleats.

It was the bottom of the fifth inning. Travis's out was the Seminoles' second. It was now up to Albie Carbone to get a mark on the scoreboard.

Albie gave it his all, but that wasn't enough. He popped out to left field for the final out.

At the top of the sixth and last inning, the bottom of the Swordtail lineup came up to bat. Their coach pulled his pitcher and put in their pinch hitter, Mike Riley.

Mike didn't let his team down. He zeroed in on Paul's first pitch and swung at it.

Crack!

It was over the left field wall for a home run. The scoreboard now read Seminoles 2, Swordtails 1.

Paul walked the next batter. With the winning run on first base, Coach McLane came out and talked to his pitcher. He signaled his infielders to stay where they were.

Whatever the coach said, Paul seemed more confident as he faced the next batter, Zang Blakewell.

The first pitch was a called strike.

The next pitch was down the middle. Zang swung at it and missed.

The next two pitches were balls.

With a 2-and-2 count, Zang seemed on edge. Travis could tell he wanted the next pitch to be a good one. The Seminole right fielder leaned in, ready for whatever came his way.

Crack!

The ball was hit to Howie's left side. The Seminole second baseman leaped for it. He managed to get under the ball just before it took off for the outfield. He was practically on his back as he flipped the ball to Travis, who was covering second base. Travis tagged the runner and scorched the ball over to first, where Seth grabbed it for the double play.

The crowd roared. Travis beamed at Howie and reached down to help him to his feet. Howie looked surprised but took Travis's hand.

Two away. Only one more out for victory.

But luck seemed to favor the Swordtails. After two hits put runners on second and third, Ron Marino sent one out to the top of the right field wall that just missed going over. The two men on base crossed the plate safely to bring the score to Swordtails 3, Seminoles 2.

Terry Wright continued the Swordtails' streak with a hit that brought Ron home. Then Jake Santos swung at and missed three quick pitches in a row for the final out.

At the bottom of the final inning, the Seminoles had to rebound in a big way or else they'd lose the play-off series. It was do or die.

Chan led off with a single to bring up Peter.

Peter struck out.

Mert came to the plate. He was walked by the Swordtails' pitcher.

Paul was up next. He was one for three at bat. This time Travis heard his conversation with the coach. He asked for a shot. "I really think I'm ready," Paul said.

Coach McLane gave him a chance to prove he was. The Seminole pitcher rewarded the coach and the team by putting one past the Swordtail first baseman for a clean hit. Only a strong throw in from their right fielder kept Chan from scoring.

With the bases loaded and only one out, Seth Franklin came up to bat.

He walked, bringing Chan in across the plate.

Next up was Howie. He popped a high one into right field that gave Mert all the time he needed to make it home. Howie was safe at first, and the score was now tied, 4–4.

"Keep it going!" called Steffi.

Travis took his place in the on-deck circle as Scoot Robertson settled down at the plate.

Scoot kept tapping off foul balls. Then he let one go by for a called strike, and the Swordtails had the second out.

Two away and bases loaded. Bottom of the last inning. Score tied. Travis could feel the pressure, from the top of his batting helmet to the bottom of his rubber cleats.

The first pitch was high and outside. Ball one.

The next was down the middle. Strike one.

The next looked like it was going to be too high. But it dropped a little just as it neared the plate.

Travis swung at it.

Crack!

The ball went sizzling down the first base line. It was heading right for Jake Santos's out-stretched glove. The Swordtail first baseman

knew he had it. He was so sure, he didn't really concentrate on bringing the ball in, and his reach was a little short. The ball hit the webbing and bobbled behind him.

That was all Travis needed. A little burst of speed put him safely on first as the winning run scored at the plate.

The umpire ruled it an error, but the Seminoles had still won the game. The series was now tied at two games apiece. The winner would be determined by the final game on Friday afternoon.

As Travis started for the dugout, he was surrounded by his teammates, who hugged him and slapped high fives with him. Fans poured down on the field from the stands and mixed with the players. This was great, but Travis wanted to get over to where Mert was, to see what he could find out. He saw the Seminole catcher on the outside edge of the crowd that just seemed to keep on growing.

"You were terrific, Travis," called a familiar voice a little way behind him. Travis turned around and saw his father heading his way. Mert, meanwhile, was disappearing off in the distance. Travis could see him going for his bicycle, but there was no way he could get near him.

When Mr. Bonelli reached Travis, he gave him a big hug. From the corner of his eye, Travis could see Mert pedaling away.

"Now don't tell me you didn't enjoy that!" said Mr. Bonelli, flashing a wide smile. "How's about a little celebration?"

Before Travis could answer, Peter shouted over to him, "Travis, we're all going down to the Dairy Bar to pig out on malteds. Come on along."

"Sure, Trav," called Howie. "Why don't you join us?"

"Yeah," said Seth. "Come on, Travis, let's get out of here."

"Uh, Dad, I'll see you at home later, okay?" said Travis.

"Even better than okay, son," said Mr. Bonelli. "Just take your time."

At the Dairy Bar, the Seminoles filled almost all the booths and half the counter. More than half the team was there. They swilled down their sodas and rehashed almost every play of the game.

There were the usual arguments about statistics, but Steffi was right there to provide the answers. Still, the differences of opinion didn't amount to much, and everyone had a good time celebrating the victory.

Peter stuck close to Travis, but a lot of the other guys talked to him. It almost felt like he really was a member of a team.

When he got home, his father called from upstairs, "Be down in a minute, Travis. I'm taking you out for dinner. Oh, there's something for you on the kitchen table."

At first, Travis thought it was another crazy note. Then he saw it was a thin envelope addressed to him. He opened it up. Inside was a letter from the horror video contest. It read:

Dear Mr. Bonelli,
Thank you for your application for the Horror Video Contest and your entry fee. We look forward to receiving your entry by the closing date of the contest.

130

Travis was dumbfounded. Could it be that whoever had stolen his videos had sent in the application *and* had paid the fee? If so, it was no ordinary thief. It was someone sending him a message.

And it could have been a lot of people. But he was starting to think he knew who it was.

14

There were no mystery calls between the fourth and fifth games of the play-offs. In fact, nothing unusual happened during that time. During practice, Mert continued to avoid Travis and Peter continued to encourage him to do his best. The coach pointed out what he was doing right and wrong. And Steffi stared at him and blew bubbles.

By the time the final game began, Travis was playing well and, most important, enjoying himself. He even allowed himself a moment to think about going to the World Series.

No question about it, there was a lot of excitement in the air as the game began.

Lou Lanahan was on the mound for the Swordtails. The Seminoles led off.

Seth stepped up to the plate. Howie crouched down in the on-deck circle.

"Come on, Seth, you can do it. Show us your stuff!" called Dutch McLane.

Steffi cracked her gum.

Seth didn't have much of a chance to show what he could do. Lanahan was still a little tense. He walked Seth with four bad pitches in a row.

At bat next, Howie saw one pitch that he couldn't resist. It was just a little low, the way he liked it. He swung, connected, and the ball soared into the outfield — but not very deep. The center fielder, Andy Reynolds, made an easy catch. Then he pegged it to first. Seth was off base and got tagged for a second out.

Scoot Robertson waited out a full count and then walked. Coming up to bat, Travis hoped he could keep things going with a hit.

But Lanahan had calmed down by now. His pitching was right on the mark. Travis barely made contact with two outside pitches for fouls. By the time he thought about swinging at a down-the-middle-scorcher, it had gone by him for a third, final, strike.

This was not the way he wanted things to go.

But he kept his cool. He had to remember it was just the first inning.

With a big goose egg on the scoreboard, the Seminoles took to the field.

"Let's go, you guys. Loosen up out there. Play tough!" shouted the coach as they settled in to play. "Let's keep them off the scoreboard."

While the first Swordtail hitter selected his bat, Travis picked up the ball Mert had tossed in front of him and threw it to Seth. It barely reached first.

"Hang in there, Travis," called Seth. He picked up the ball and threw it to Scoot.

"Nice and easy," said Scoot, firing it over to Howie.

"Heads up!" called Howie. He faked flipping it to Paul Farley on the mound but lobbed it over to Travis.

The Seminole shortstop made a big display of snagging the easy catch, doffed his cap, and took a bow. He had a big smile on his face.

As he looked around, he saw the other guys all smiling back.

"Let's play ball!" called the ump.

The Swordtails were also wound up about playing this final game of the series. They tried too
hard and swung too often at bad pitches. Even
though two of their batters got on base, they
couldn't manage to bring them home. At the end
of the first inning, there was still no score.

In the second inning, a few Swordtail errors
and a few walks by Lanahan put some excitement
into the game. Both Peter and Mert crossed the
plate standing up to put the Seminoles ahead,
2–0.

But the Swordtails came right back. Terry
Wright led off with a home run over the left field
wall. Then Jake Santos cracked a line drive down
the middle for a single.

Things calmed down a bit after Shelly Ross and
Lou Lanahan both went down swinging.

The top of the Swordtail roster then came up
as Stan marched up to the plate. Travis could see
that he was just aching to hit a long ball. He
backed up a few steps, just in case.

It didn't matter. The long ball Stan hit was
way out of his reach. It sailed over the right field
wall.

A strikeout by Zang Blakewell ended the inning. The Swordtails were now ahead, 3–2.

Coach McLane tried to stir his team up before they went to bat in the third inning.

"Keep your eyes on the ball," he told them. "Clear everything else out of your heads. One pitch at a time, okay?"

Howie led off, looking determined to make up for his double play in the first inning. Lanahan started off with a pitch that sailed by the batter's nose. Probably another walk, Travis thought as he watched from the on-deck circle.

But the next pitch was well within range, and Howie swung at it.

Crack!

A ground ball in the slot between short and third. Howie arrived at first base grinning from ear to ear.

Next up, Travis settled into position at the plate. If a good pitch comes, he thought, I'll go for it. But I'll probably end up walking. As long as I don't go after any really bad ones.

The first three pitches were, indeed, bad. It looked as though his prediction about walking would come through. But with a 3-and-0 count, Lanahan surprised him with a slow pitch right down the middle that Travis couldn't resist. He swung and connected.

It was a pop fly toward the second baseman, who ran for it. Travis was pretty sure it was going to be an easy catch. He put down his bat and ambled toward first base at a slow trot.

But the Swordtail fielder was off stride, and the ball bounced off his glove. Seeing that Travis hadn't gotten very far, he recovered quickly. He grabbed the ball and pegged it to Jake Santos, who had plenty of time to make the out at first.

There were boos from the stands as Travis returned to the dugout. Some of the guys tried to cheer him up, but he was miserable. He tried to avoid the coach by slinking down in the far corner.

He hadn't reckoned with Steffi.

She worked her way over to him and told him what she thought. "You're either lazy or dumb, Travis," she whispered angrily. "One or the other, you're not doing much to help us win!"

Travis didn't want the rest of the guys to hear

him fighting with the scorekeeper. He turned his back to them as he replied, "I'm doing the best I can. Besides, what's it to you, anyhow?"

"I'll tell you what," she said. "This is my shot at getting to the World Series, too. Coach McLane said I could go if the Seminoles won."

"You'd do just about anything to go, wouldn't you?" said Travis.

"If I were out there, I sure would play my heart out," Steffi answered. "I wouldn't relax for a minute."

"That's not what I'm talking about," said Travis.

"What do you mean, then?" she asked.

"I mean strange phone calls, mysterious notes, stolen tapes," he said.

"I don't know what you're talking about," she said, looking away from him.

"Oh, yes, you do. And you knew about the contest, too, 'cause I told you about it," he continued.

"I don't remember," she said.

"You sent in the application. You probably put real money in with it instead of a check, so it couldn't be traced," he went on. "And you got the idea about the phone calls from *Sorry, Wrong*

Number, the movie I was telling Peter about. You heard us talking that day. And I'll bet the note I got was a lot like one of the 'gloom-and-doom' fortunes you get with your bubble gum!" Travis tapped her scorecard. "That note was printed nice and neat, too, just like your roster."

"You're nuts," she said. "Besides, you don't have any real proof."

"I don't need any," he said. "I've figured it all out, and I'm sure it was you."

"Sure, sure," she said. She pretended she wasn't interested, but Travis went on.

"You can tell when I'm home because your house looks over at ours," he said. "And you can see the light in my workshop. If the light was off, you knew I wasn't up there. That's how you could sneak in and grab my tapes."

Steffi's face grew redder and redder.

"Well, I had to do something," she finally admitted.

"What do you mean?" he asked.

"I just wanted you to concentrate on playing baseball and to become a real member of the Seminoles," she explained. "You spent too much time on those tapes and not enough time getting to know the rest of team. And then that contest came up. Nobody could seem to get through to you. So I figured maybe I could scare you into being serious about the play-offs."

"What about that call Mert said he got? Was that for real?" he asked.

"Yeah, I did that, too," she confessed. "I was going to call everyone who wasn't playing up to steam. But I got worried that someone might recognize my voice, so I stopped. I wasn't even going to give you a second call. But you needed it."

"Why?"

"You never listened to me," she said. "Whenever I tried to get you to talk about baseball, you blabbed away about horror movies. You kept holing up in that garage workshop. Everyone figured you just didn't care about the series. I had to do something to get you out of there!"

"I . . . I just took it for granted you all knew how much I loved baseball," he said. "I started to work on my videos to relax, but I guess you're right. That sort of got to be too much. I shouldn't have even bothered with the darn contest."

"No, you can still do the contest," she said. "After the play-offs are over. That's why I sent in the application. I was afraid you'd tear it up when you saw the tapes were gone. I'll give them back right after the game."

"The game," he said. "That's what's really important right now. We're not out of it yet."

15

As he watched Albie Carbone at the plate, Travis thought long and hard about what Steffi had said. He recalled Howie's surprised look when he had held out a hand to help him up. Did the other guys really think I'm a cold fish? he wondered. That I don't care about baseball? Well, they're in for a surprise, I guess!

Albie failed to get a hit for the second time in this game. He slouched back into the dugout.

"No sweat, Albie," said Travis, clapping him on the shoulder. "You'll get 'im next time."

A few of the players looked over at Travis with surprised smiles.

Chan managed to belt one to the hole between left and center. That got him to second base. Howie advanced to third, where he held up.

Peter Hooper was now at bat with two outs. He looked as though he were in a hurry to get it over with. He swung at the first two pitches and missed them both by a mile.

Travis got up and shouted toward the plate. "Eye on the ball, Pete! You can do it!"

The next pitch was a ball. So were the next three. Peter smiled toward the dugout as he trotted down to first base.

The bases were now loaded. Mert moved from the on-deck circle to the batter's box.

As the burly catcher took a few practice swings, Travis started a chant: "Fa-rish! Fa-rish! Fa-rish!"

The Seminole bench took it up. They were followed by their fans in the stands. Travis looked over and saw his mother and father waving and cheering along.

Mert watched the first outside pitch go by. Then he popped off two foul balls into the first base stands. The next pitch was the one he really wanted. He swung with all his might.

Crack!

The sky-high ball headed right for the center field wall and stopped just short of going over. Andy Reynolds grabbed it on a bounce and pegged it to second. The relay to home was too late. Howie scored to tie up the game, 3–3.

The Seminoles gave him a big welcome as he crossed the plate.

Paul was up next. Coach McLane called him over. After a moment of discussion, Paul stepped to the plate.

As soon as the first decent pitch came his way, Paul bunted the ball. He tried to aim it toward third base, but he leaned in too far and it curved down the first base line. He was tagged out half-way to the base.

It was the third out.

Still, the Seminoles held themselves a little taller as they took to the field. They had shown that the game was, indeed, far from over.

Paul quickly put away the first two Swordtails who came up to bat. The only balls they managed to hit ended up in foul territory. One went down swinging, the other on a called strike.

Ron Marino managed to squeeze a single out of a bad bounce that wiggled away from Scoot Robertson. The next batter, Terry Wright, tried to do the same thing. But Travis was fast on his toes and caught it in time to flip the ball to Howie for the out at second.

The Seminoles were showing strength on the field as well as at the plate. Travis felt great about being part of their tough new push toward a victory.

During the next two innings, both sides really dug in. Each managed to get another run on the scoreboard. At the end of the fifth inning, it read Swordtails 4, Seminoles 4.

"You're up, Scoot," called Steffi as the team came into the dugout for the final inning. "Travis, get set — you're next."

Scoot took his place in the batter's box.

"Come on, Scoot!" shouted the Seminoles' fans. "Blast it out of there!"

Lou Lanahan eyed the batter. He looked for the signal from Shelly and shook his head. He must have liked the next choice since he nodded his agreement.

He wound up and hurled the ball.

Scoot swung at it — and connected.

Crack!

A high fly ball rose up above the third base

line. Ron Marino called for it and put it away for the first out.

"Your turn, Travis! Make 'em eat dirt!" shouted Howie.

The Seminoles joined him in cheering on their star shortstop.

"Tra-vis! Tra-vis!"

Travis moved into the batter's box. He swung his bat around his head to loosen up. As he waited for the first pitch, he looked out toward short. It reminded him of the practice when Mert was out there.

Stan Weinberg, the Swordtail shortstop, didn't look any more ready than Mert had. He was more standing up than crouching. That was the spot, Travis decided.

He could see Lou watching for the signal from Shelly. It took three before he nodded. Then he wound up and delivered.

The pitch was wide.

"Ball!" called the ump.

Travis stepped back and tapped the bat against his cleats. Back in the box, he saw Lou ready with his next pitch.

Down it came. "Ball two!"

The next pitch was almost over Travis's head.

"Ball three!"

Was he going to walk? Or was he going to be tricked into going for a bad pitch?

"Wait him out, Travis!"

"He's afraid of you!"

"You can do it, slugger!"

The shouts of encouragement from the Seminole dugout fired him up. He stood there with his bat held high, his legs close together.

The next pitch sped toward the plate.

Crack!

It was a solid drive just over short. Stan wasn't ready for it or he'd have grabbed it on a leap. But it sailed over his head and Travis arrived safe at first.

"Go, Seminoles, go!" shouted the fans.

Albie Carbone came up to bat. He had gone hitless all day. This time his luck changed. A wobbler down the third base line took him safely to first. Travis advanced to second.

The next batter, Chan Lee, struck out.

Then Peter Hooper came up to bat.

"Let's go, Peter!" called Travis from second base. "Take me all the way!"

Peter fanned the first two pitches. He connected on the third.

It was a ground ball down the third base line. Ron made a leap for it, but it bounced off his glove toward short. Travis passed him scrambling for the ball.

By the time Ron got a hold of it and made the peg home, Travis had outraced the ball. He crossed the plate to a roaring welcome from the team and the fans. The Seminoles were now ahead by one run.

Mert tried to keep the rally going, but his line drive to the second baseman gave the team their final out.

Travis stepped in his way as Mert went to pick up his protective gear.

"Don't let it get you down," Travis said to him. "You've played a heck of a game. Now all we have to do is hold them."

He thrust his hand forward for a high five and Mert automatically gave him one. Travis was surprised at how easy it was to act friendly to Mert.

148

Both players took to the field with happy expressions on their faces.

Paul had his work cut out for him. To start things off, he faced Karim Kadar. The Swordtail left fielder was their strongest hitter all season. He'd had a great series so far.

Karim found an inside curveball he liked and swung at it.

He was too far under it. His bat tipped it, and the ball rose high above the plate. Mert was right there. He caught it for the first out.

The next batter, Ron Marino, went down swinging. Two away.

All the Swordtail hopes now rested on Terry Wright. He'd hit their only home run during this game. Travis wondered if he would do it again.

Coach McLane signaled his team to play Terry deep. Travis backed up to the edge of the track. He crouched down but stayed ready to spring up in an instant if he had to.

Terry let the first two pitches go by for a 2-and-0 count. He swung at the next pitch and missed. The Swordtail fans groaned.

Paul took Mert's first signal for the next pitch. He toed the rubber, wound up, and delivered.

It was a fastball down the middle. Terry was ready for it and swung.

Crack!

He was on his way toward first as the ball soared toward the center field wall. It hit the top and bounced back onto the field. By this time, Terry was rounding second base.

Chan Lee pegged the ball to second, but it got by Howie.

Travis was behind him and stopped the ball before it went any farther.

Terry had decided to go all the way. He had all his steam working as he sped down the line toward home plate.

Mert was crouched and ready for the peg. Travis spun and hurled the ball in his direction.

Smack! Mert caught the ball right in the center of his mitt. With lightning quick speed, he swung to tag Terry as he slid into home.

"Out!"

The fans exploded in the stands, cheering and applauding. The winning combination of Travis

Bonelli and Mert Farish had saved the day. Final score: Seminoles 5, Swordtails 4. The Seminoles were the official league champions.

The field filled up quickly with fans who poured down from the stands to congratulate the team when they came off the field. Steffi was standing on top of the bench shouting and cheering. She caught Travis's eye and gave him a big thumbs-up sign. He signaled the same back to her.

Coach McLane barely managed to herd his players toward the dugout to shake their hands.

"You guys were all great," he told them. "I'm mighty proud of each and every one of you. You've earned that trip to the World Series by playing hard and working together as a team." He glanced briefly at Travis and then at Mert. Then he cleared his throat.

"Now I'm afraid I have some bad news," he went on. "As some of you may know, I'm going to be coaching football this fall. Unfortunately, my coaching duties begin the same week as the World Series. Now, as sorry as I am to not be going to the greatest matchup since the Seminoles-Swordtails, I'm even sorrier to report that I haven't found anyone able to go in my place. Unless I do, I don't think . . . well, you can't go by yourselves — you know that."

Travis felt sick. A quick glance around the dugout showed him the rest of the team wasn't feeling much better.

"Hey, did I hear right?" a voice outside the dugout asked. Travis looked up to see his father standing there with Mrs. Bonelli and the Hoopers.

"You're looking for someone to escort this group of guys —"

"And me, too," piped up Steffi.

"And one special scorekeeper," Mr. Bonelli added. "We ought to be able to do something about that. Matter of fact, why don't we go with them?" he asked his wife.

"There's enough time for me to arrange my schedule," said Mrs. Bonelli. "What about your bowling league?" she asked.

"We didn't make the play-offs," he announced with a smile toward Bernie Hooper, who laughed. Tom Farish, standing next to him, shook his head.

"Besides," Mr. Bonelli went on, "how often do we get a chance to go to the World Series?"

There were cheers from the Bonellis. The coach agreed to arrange things with Hoagy's.

"Now, how about a celebration?" suggested Peter's dad. "The Seminoles' parents will spring for a party down at the Dairy Bar. Anyone interested?"

The loud sound of agreement filled the air.

"And afterward," said Mr. Bonelli, "anyone who wants can come over to our house and see *my* favorite video."

"Oh, no, not one of Travis's horror movies," groaned Mert Farish.

"No, this is one I put together," said Mr. Bonelli. "It's all the dumb things Travis has done on the baseball diamond since he was a little kid. I've been taping his games for all those years."

"This one, too," said Mrs. Bonelli, pointing at the camcorder in her husband's hands.

"Okay, Dad," said Travis. "But after you put in today's game, I'm going to add one more thing."

"What's that?" asked Steffi. "A picture of my scorecard?"

"No," he said. *"The End."*

How many of these Matt Christopher sports classics have you read?

❑ Baseball Flyhawk
❑ Baseball Pals
❑ The Basket Counts
❑ Catch That Pass!
❑ Catcher with a Glass Arm
❑ Challenge at Second Base
❑ The Counterfeit Tackle
❑ The Diamond Champs
❑ Dirt Bike Racer
❑ Dirt Bike Runaway
❑ Face-Off
❑ Football Fugitive
❑ The Fox Steals Home
❑ The Great Quarterback Switch
❑ Hard Drive to Short
❑ The Hockey Machine
❑ Ice Magic
❑ Johnny Long Legs
❑ The Kid Who Only Hit Homers
❑ Little Lefty
❑ Long Shot for Paul
❑ Long Stretch at First Base
❑ Look Who's Playing First Base
❑ Miracle at the Plate
❑ No Arm in Left Field
❑ Pressure Play
❑ Red-Hot Hightops
❑ Return of the Home Run Kid
❑ Run, Billy, Run
❑ Shortstop from Tokyo
❑ Skateboard Tough
❑ Soccer Halfback
❑ The Submarine Pitch
❑ Supercharged Infield
❑ Tackle Without a Team
❑ Tight End
❑ Too Hot to Handle
❑ Touchdown for Tommy
❑ Tough to Tackle
❑ Undercover Tailback
❑ Wingman on Ice
❑ The Year Mom Won the Pennant

All available in paperback from Little, Brown and Company

Join the Matt Christopher Fan Club!

To become an official member of the Matt Christopher Fan Club,
send a business-size (9 1/2 x 4") self-addressed stamped envelope and $1.00 to:

Matt Christopher Fan Club
c/o Little, Brown and Company
34 Beacon Street
Boston, MA 02108